"Get out of he
just get out!"

Clare's voice was hoarse with anger.

Rourke came to a halt, the contempt deepening in his eyes. "I have no intention of coming near you, Clare. I'm still not the right man to try your teasing ways on. Listening to you just now, with your loving fiancé, brought all the memories back." He looked her over consideringly, almost insultingly. "You're thinner than you were then, more haughty, too—"

"I've grown up," she corrected distantly.

His mouth twisted. "You always were grown up, it just took me a while to realize *how* grown up. You should know by now that you don't need to *ask* men to make love to you—they can't help themselves."

CAROLE MORTIMER
is also the author of these

Harlequin Presents

Many of these books are available at your local bookseller.

For a free catalog listing all titles currently available,
send your name and address to:

HARLEQUIN READER SERVICE
1440 South Priest Drive, Tempe, AZ 85281
Canadian address: Stratford, Ontario N5A 6W2

CAROLE MORTIMER

golden fever

Harlequin Books

TORONTO • NEW YORK • LOS ANGELES • LONDON
AMSTERDAM • PARIS • SYDNEY • HAMBURG
STOCKHOLM • ATHENS • TOKYO • MILAN

For
John and Matthew

Harlequin Presents first edition March 1983
ISBN 0-373-10579-7

Original hardcover edition published in 1982
by Mills & Boon Limited

CHAPTER ONE

It was amazing how Los Angeles airport never seemed to change, just as the people never seemed to change. Clare had lost count of the amount of times she had landed here, and yet each time it looked like the same people milling around, the same engrossed faces, the eagerness of a holidaymaker, the world-weary one of the businessman.

What category did she fall into? She wasn't a holidaymaker, that was for sure. The days of her carefree youth spent on Malibu Beach were long gone. She was here to work, so that probably put her in the latter category.

And yet she felt as if she had come home. The last five years of living in London might not have happened. She felt like the eighteen-year-old she had been then, just newly left school, the whole world at her feet. Only she hadn't seen the whole world, only——

No! She wouldn't think of him. She never thought of him now, or of the time she had spent with him.

'The baggage!' Her voice was sharp as she turned to the man walking at her side.

Harvey Pryce looked his usual calm, unruffled self, not at all like a man who had just spent over nine hours on an aeroplane. And why should he?—he had been asleep five minutes after take-off, only waking up in time to freshen up, change his jacket, and leave the plane.

And Clare had spent the same time wondering if she had made a mistake in agreeing to do this film. Of course, when she had accepted the part she hadn't realised that some of the filming would take place in Long Beach. If she had known that she wouldn't even have looked at the script.

She was still running away, she knew that. And there wasn't a damn thing she could do about it. Just to think of Rourke made her feel like the gauche innocent she had been then, and considering she was known for her coolness now that was some admission.

'I'll get it,' Harvey answered her statement, striding confidently over to pick up the single cases they had each brought with them.

Clare waited, immune to the admiring glances she was receiving, a tall slender woman in a golden-yellow dress, a wide white leather belt secured about her narrow waist, the straightness of the skirt emphasising the long length of her tanned legs. Her hair hung straight and golden to her shoulders, her face youthfully beautiful, her eyes golden beneath winged brows. 'Golden Lady', the press had nicknamed her, and Harvey, as her manager, saw to it that she kept to that image.

'Miss Anderson?' A young man stood in front of her, a boy of eighteen or nineteen, his flushed eagerness showing his youth. 'It *is* Clare Anderson, isn't it?' he asked uncertainly as she remained silent.

She looked at him coolly, the perfection of her face showing no emotion. 'Yes?' Her voice was low and husky, naturally so, and not affected as so many so-called friends liked to think.

'Oh, boy!' His face lit up. Like so many of his contemporaries he was dressed casually, in faded denims and a tee-shirt, with not a care in the world other than having a good time. And L.A. was certainly the place for that.

Clare envied him, feeling about fifty years old when faced with his youthful enthusiasm. It certainly *felt* as if she had lived that long sometimes—the constant barrage of work, the different locations, the different fellow actors to work with. And when she wasn't working she was attending the parties Harvey claimed she had to go to so that she was never forgotten, was always in the public eye.

Only Harvey remained the same, safe, reliable Harvey, who would sell his soul to get *his* star the leading role, the best publicity. And *she* was that star!

And she wore his ring, a large chunky diamond that weighed heavily on her long slender finger. The ring had been there a little over a year now, and so far they had made no plans of putting a plain gold one at its side.

'Can I have your autograph?' the young boy was asking now.

'I—Sorry?' she frowned, too preoccupied to be aware of what he was saying to her.

'This young man would like your autograph, Clare.' Harvey materialised at her side, instantly taking charge of the situation, leaving the porter to struggle along with their suitcases, carrying only the briefcase that had accompanied him on the plane. He flicked open the briefcase, and a photograph of Clare miraculously appeared from its depths. 'Here,' he handed it to her to sign, censure in his frowning blue eyes.

Clare bit her bottom lip, knowing she was being less than gracious, favouring the boy with a smile designed to dazzle—knowing she had succeeded when he flushed his pleasure.

She couldn't be more than four or five years older than this lad, and yet she felt miles apart from him, knew that her way of life, the glitter, the falseness, had given her a sophistication that more than matched Harvey's thirty-five years.

But she was going off at a tangent again, her thoughts constantly wandering today. Once again she smiled at the waiting boy, and took a gold pen from her handbag. 'Who shall I write it to?' she queried softly.

'Nick,' he said eagerly, watching as she scrawled his name across the bottom of the photograph, accompanying it with her own. 'Thanks,' he accepted it gratefully, disappearing into the crowd as suddenly as he had appeared.

Harvey took hold of Clare's arm, guiding her outside with a firmness that dared even the most ardent fan to accost them, ushering her into the waiting limousine as a crowd began to gather about them.

'What's the matter with you? he demanded as the car glided smoothly away from the excited people staring in the windows. 'You almost didn't give that boy your autograph,' he added sternly. 'A couple of stories in the press of you not appreciating your fans and you'll have your nickname changed to "the Golden Bitch"!'

Clare smiled, with her lips only, her eyes remaining coolly golden. 'That "fan" walked off with my pen,' she told him sweetly.

Irritation furrowed his handsome face. 'You should have stopped him——'

'And risked my image?' she taunted softly, the smile still curving her peach-coloured lips. Her make-up was very light, her lashes naturally dark, her skin the colour of honey and glowing with good health. Only the dullness of her eyes showed her dissatisfaction with her life, the questioning of whether, now that she had her fame and fortune, that were all there were to life.

'The pen was gold, Clare,' Harvey snapped.

She shrugged. 'Gold for the Golden Lady.'

'But I gave it to you!'

Her expression instantly changed to one of contrition, her hand moving to rest lightly on his thigh. 'I'm sorry, darling. I'll make my—thoughtlessness up to you later,' she added provocatively.

His frown told her that this didn't please him either, the look he shot in the direction of their driver showing her the reason why it didn't. He firmly took her hand in his, shaking his head.

Clare turned to look out of the window, at the palm trees that grew along the roadside, the abundance of tropical plants. The weather was hot and humid, a smog shrouding the city like a blanket, looking almost like a London fog. Harvey was already beginning to look hot and uncomfortable, perspiration starting to bead his forehead. Of course the grey suit he wore was more suited to an English summer than the humidity of L.A., but then the weather had been cool in England for August.

Clare frowned as the limousine turned on to the all-too-familiar Sunset Boulevard. 'Where are we going, Harvey?' she asked sharply, emotion at last etched into her face.

'Your mother——'

'Tell the driver to turn the car around, Harvey,' she ordered stiffly, sitting tensely in her seat.

'But, Clare——'

'Now!' she bit out, her eyes flashing deeply gold.

'But your mother——'

'Can wait. And she can go on waiting.'

'Clare——'

'Will you tell the driver or do I have to do it myself?' Her tone brooked no further argument.

Harvey sighed his impatience, leaning forward to issue new instructions to the driver. Clare watched him with angry eyes. Her fiancé was very good-looking in an executive sort of way—blond hair almost as gold as her own was kept short to control its tendency to curl, his eyes were the blue of the sea, his nose short and straight, his mouth thin, unsmiling now, his jaw thrust out aggressively, his body slender, the sort of body that wore clothes well.

Harvey had taken control of her career—and her life—three years ago, and she very rarely opposed him in this way. But about her mother she would remain adamant.

He sat back, still angry with her. 'I've told him to take us to the hotel,' he told her tightly.

The hotel was the ship *Queen Mary*, and it seemed strange to think of an over eighty-thousand-ton ship as a hotel. Moored at Long Beach since 1967, it was now run as a hotel. Clare had never travelled on her while she had been in service as a cruise liner, and she was curious to see the huge ship that had been saved in this unique way from being broken up for scrap.

But she couldn't let Harvey off this lightly. 'When did you speak to my mother?' she wanted to know.

'I called her——'

'*You* did?' Her eyes widened in exasperation. 'Why would you call my mother?'

'She is going to be my mother-in-law——'

'That's never bothered you before.' Her mouth twisted.

He flushed his irritation at this unexpected show of anger from her. 'It doesn't bother me now, it wouldn't bother any man to have Carlene Walters as his mother-in-law.'

Clare could hear the admiration in his voice, and she prickled resentfully. 'Then maybe you should be marrying her and not me.'

His eyes narrowed. 'Now you're being ridiculous!'

She sighed, smoothing the yellow dress down the long length of her thighs. 'What did you talk to her about?' she asked casually.

'You, mainly,' Harvey was eager to explain. 'She really wants to see you, Clare.'

'I'll bet!' Her tone was derisive.

'Clare, please,' he sighed. 'It's been years now——'

Once again she turned to look out of the window, no longer listening to him. She knew exactly how long it was since she had last seen her mother, could have told Harvey down to the last minute exactly how long it was since she had walked out of her mother's house determined never to see her again—and nothing had happened in the last five years to change her mind about that.

'Clare, are you listening to me?' Harvey asked impatiently.

She didn't even turn. 'No.'

'You're being unreasonable——'

Now she did turn, more angry than she could remember being in a long time. 'I've never tried to interfere in your life, in any way,' her voice was cold. 'Now you can manage my career, you even have a say in my future, but my past—and that includes my mother—is none of your business.'

He looked as if she had mortally wounded him. 'Clare!' His tone was reproachful.

God, what was wrong with her! Ever since this L.A. location had been mentioned she had been as tense as a coiled spring, and taking it out on Harvey wasn't going to make the next few weeks any easier to bear.

'I'm sorry, darling,' she said warmly, bending forward to kiss him lightly on the mouth, deliberately pressing her breasts against his chest, knowing that he could see their gentle swell as he looked down at her. He was flushed with pleasure by the time she moved to her own side of the seat.

She had known of Harvey's physical interest in her from the first, but for the first eighteen months they had both ignored it. Harvey had been suffering from a broken relationship with the girl he had managed before her, and she had been suffering emotionally herself. But time had healed both of their raw emotions, and soon Harvey was making it clear that when she was ready for an emotional involvement he would be waiting for her.

And he had been. Eighteen months ago she had given him the green light, and he hadn't lost a moment, pursuing her relentlessly, only relaxing that pursuit when he had his ring on her finger. They were perfectly suited, and Harvey never demanded more than she wanted to give, despite the fact that he had had a deep physical relationship with Shara Morgan, the girl who had so deeply hurt him. So far their own relationship hadn't deepened to intimacy, but Clare knew Harvey was waiting for the day—or night, that it did.

They were on the freeway now, well on their way to Long Beach, and the three distinctive funnels of the *Queen*

Mary were visible long before they stopped at the car park gate to enter into the docking area.

She was a beautiful ship, still regal despite no longer sailing the seas she had been designed to sail. They drove past Londontowne, a small replica of some of the older style shops and cafés in London, England, driving up to the entrance of the hotel, an addition to the hotel built on the dockside, a lift just inside to transport guests up to the reception area.

Harvey stepped out on to the pavement as the driver held the door open for them, holding Clare's hand as she stepeed out beside him. 'Makes you feel homesick, doesn't it?' he grinned in the direction of the red double-decker bus parked at the roadside.

Clare smiled her thanks at their driver before he quietly disappeared, then turned to look at the regality of the *Queen Mary*, at once feeling the pull of her beauty, a certain feeling of going back in time. Lords and ladies, film stars, and political figures had travelled on her in the past, and it could be felt in her graciousness, in her mellow beauty.

'I love it,' Clare said breathlessly, her eyes shining.

'Like a small part of England, isn't it?' Harvey smiled as six young men in Grenadier Guards uniforms marched to the sentry boxes at the side of the dock for the Changing of the Guard, a purely tourist gimmick.

It was like a small part of England, the country Clare now considered home even though her passport clearly stated she was an American citizen. Educated in England most of her life, only occasional holidays spent in California, she even spoke with an English accent. Yes, this was like a small part of England, and maybe the next few weeks weren't going to be so bad after all; the role of Caroline was certainly an interesting one.

Clare walked beside Harvey with graceful elegance as the porter brought the lift down to take them and their luggage up to the reception area; even the staff uniforms were like that of the British Navy.

The reception was a hive of activity, people checking in and checking out, but nevertheless Harvey was attended to almost immediately, and all the time she was dealing with him the receptionist sent interested looks in Clare's direction. Clare returned the smile, used to such attention now, although she still found it rather unnerving. The last two films she had made, and starred in, had been box-office hits, making her face known world-wide.

To Harvey her working in California, only miles from Hollywood, was the highlight of her career, and he meant to take advantage of the fact. She had yet to tell him she had no intention of going to any of the parties that would go on there during their stay. She was determined not to see her mother, not even accidentally, and there was hardly a party in Hollywood that her mother didn't attend.

Another porter had taken charge of their luggage now, smiling admiringly at Clare as he took them to their rooms. Clare had been given the Royal Suite with Harvey's stateroom just down the corridor.

'Of course this isn't all of it,' the young porter, dressed in a pure white uniform, explained as he unloaded her case from the trolley. 'This suite used to be five rooms, two bedrooms with adjoining bathroom, and a lounge area, but for practical purposes it's been divided into two suites with one bedroom each and a small lounge area.'

Clare looked about her admiringly, loving the charm and elegance that oozed out of the original woodwork that had gone into the ship's building in the early thirties.

'Some of the furniture is original too.' The porter saw her appreciative looks.

She smiled at him, unconscious of her glowing beauty her long legs in the high-heeled sandals, the slenderness of her waist emphasised by the wide belt, the latter also showing the fullness of her breasts and her shapely hips.

She wore little jewellery, a slender gold chain about her throat, a matching bracelet about her wrist, and of course her engagement ring.

'But not the television,' she teased huskily.

'No,' he smiled agreement. 'Although most people expect them nowadays. I hope you enjoy your stay with us, Miss Anderson.'

'I'm sure I shall.' She tipped him, closing the door behind him as he left with Harvey to show him his room.

Jason had chosen the location spots, and he had chosen well, she could see that. The film, the story of a couple, an English girl and a German man, who met on this ship during the pre-war years and fell in love, only to meet again fifteen years later, when Caroline was married to someone else, would be better for being filmed on board the actual ship. Of course some of it had been changed over the years, and would have to be mocked up or filmed in a studio, but the majority of filming could be done here, on the *Queen Mary*, the very ship where the romance was supposed to have taken place.

Jason Faulkner wasn't just the director of the film, he was also her co-star, would play the part of Gunther to her Caroline. She had filmed only once with him before, when he was the star and she had only a very small supporting role. But even then she had found him unfailingly polite, with a patience and tolerance for his fellow actors that made working with him a pleasure. The preliminary work they had done on the film so far had been made easier because of his complete professionalism.

A knock sounded on her door just as she was considering taking a shower. As she had guessed, it was Harvey.

'I've ordered you some tea.' He came in without being invited, sitting down on the sofa. 'Good God, what's that?' He looked aghast at the fireplace.

Clare had to smile at his expression. 'One of the original electric fireplaces, I believe,' she drawled.

Harvey frowned. 'Have I got one in my room? I suppose I have. I didn't take the time to look. Do you think it works?'

'I have no idea,' she shrugged, each movement made with unconscious grace. 'But I doubt if it would ever be needed here even if it does.'

'No,' he acknowledged ruefully. 'By the way, there was a message for you at the desk.'

'There was?' she said sharply.

'Mm. Apparently the whole cast is to meet in the Windsor Room at two o'clock.'

'The Windsor Room?'

He nodded. 'It's two floors down, on R Deck—I checked.' He shook his head. 'I can't get over the fact that this is actually a boat.'

'Ship,' Clare automatically corrected.

'Ship, then,' he shrugged. 'Do you know we actually move up and down with the tide? I thought the damned thing would be secured somehow, but I'm told we're floating in forty feet of water, with a draught of thirty-three feet. I wonder if you can get seasick without even moving . . .?'

'Oh, Harvey,' she burst out laughing at his woebegone expression, 'don't be silly!'

'Well, I feel as if I'm swaying all the time!'

'That's probably the flight,' she teased. 'A couple of hours' sleep and you'll feel fine.'

'No time for sleep.' He stood up decisively. 'A shower and a change of clothes, lunch, and then you have to go to the Windsor Room.'

'You don't have to accompany me to lunch,' she excused gently, seeing that he did actually look a little pale. 'We can meet at dinner time.'

He seemed to hesitate. 'It's only twelve now. I don't like to leave you on your own all that time.'

'I won't be on my own,' she smiled. 'By the time I've

showered and had lunch it will be time to go to the meeting. I'll probably rest myself after that.'

'Why not rest for an hour now?' Harvey suggested. 'You have a couple of hours, and you can get a snack lunch in the Capstan Restaurant later.'

She gave him a puzzled look. 'You seem to know a lot about the ship considering we've only been here a few minutes!'

He gave a sheepish smile. 'I read up on the Room Service while I was in my room. I happened to see the different restaurants on board at the same time. I thought I might just have a sandwich in my room.'

'Good idea,' she nodded. 'Maybe I'll do the same.'

But when it came to it she didn't feel like staying in her room. Her shower had refreshed her, her hair was newly washed and gleaming, her dress a deep shade of pink, off the shoulders, resting provocatively on her uptilted breasts. Her legs were bare, deeply tanned, the pink of her high-heeled sandals exactly matching the colour of her dress. As a child she had hated her height, always being taller than her classmates, but now it was a definite asset. Most of the popular actresses of her generation seemed to be taller than average, a new era in sex symbols.

She hated that description of herself, but was well aware of the fact that the media referred to her as such, that some even compared her with her still popular mother.

The latter she detested even more than being referred to as a sex-symbol, seeing no resemblance between her slender coolness and the kittenish image her mother cultivated.

At times she even managed to forget Carlene Walters was her mother, and she felt sure she had tried to do the same thing. After all, when you had stopped ageing at thirty-six it was a little hard to admit to having a twenty-three-year-old daughter. Her press releases always claimed she had been a child bride, but even so . . .

Damn! She hadn't wanted to think about her mother, had studiously avoided doing so on the flight over here. Why on earth Harvey had had to call her she had no idea. No, that wasn't strictly true. She did know. Her mother was still the undisputed Queen of Hollywood, and Harvey hoped to use her influence while they were here.

She couldn't altogether blame him, after all it was his job to see that her career reached its highest pinnacle. But she drew the line at asking her mother for anything. She had reached this stage in her career, and she wasn't being conceited when she knew that she was quite successful, without any help from her mother, and she would continue to do so.

She could hear someone moving about in the adjoining suite, whistling to themselves as they seemed to be preparing for lunch. Thoughts of the latter reminded her that it was almost one o'clock, and it was some time since she had eaten anything but plane food.

The Capstan appeared to be quite busy, but the boy at the door found her a vacant table near the window. The view of the harbour was breathtaking, with ships waiting in line to dock.

Clare had quite a view of Long Beach from the porthole windows in her suite on the other side of the ship, everywhere looking very white and clean from here, the sea a greyish-blue, and several people were out in speedboats when she had last looked out.

A young boy came to take her order, and she looked up and smiled at him, the smile deepening to sympathy as he recognised her and instantly dropped the menu on the floor.

He fumbled picking it up again. 'I—Sorry.' He licked his lips nervously. 'It was just that for a moment you——' He frowned, shaking his head. 'You *are* Clare Anderson, aren't you?' he queried disbelievingly.

Maybe she would have been wiser to have eaten in her room after all; she didn't relish the thought of being on show as she ate. If this boy had recognised her then other people would too.

She didn't bother to look at the menu, neither confirming nor denying the boy's statement. 'Could I have a chicken salad?' she requested softly, finding the boy's stares a little unnerving.

'I'm sure you could,' he nodded eagerly. 'Are you here with the others making the movie?'

'Yes,' she sighed, realising he wasn't going to give up.

He nodded again. 'There are several other people in here that are going to be in it too. I'm David, by the way. If you need anything, just ask.'

'Thanks, I will.'

She accepted the offered coffee, glad when David at last left. By tonight she was going to be dead on her feet; the time difference would have caught up with her by then, although right now she didn't feel too bad.

'Clare!'

She turned with a frown, her tension relaxing as she recognised Rena Dawes. Rena was to play her sister in the film. The two of them had been at drama school together, and Clare had been delighted when she found the two of them were to be working together.

'How lovely to see you,' she said warmly. 'Can you join me?'

'Of course,' Rena was a pretty girl of her own age, also blonde, with a mischievous grin never far from the surface. She sat in the chair next to Clare. 'I was sitting over the other side of the room with some of the camera crew, but their talk got a bit technical for me.'

Clare laughed. 'It gets too technical for them sometimes!'

Her friend looked at her appreciatively. 'I don't have to ask how life's been treating you—you look marvellous. And where's that handsome fiancé of yours?'

'Resting. Have you eaten?'

'Not yet.'

Rena ordered her meal, and the two girls chatted as

they ate, recalling old times; the two of them had once shared a flat for a few weeks.

'Whatever happened to that boy Alan you were always trying to evade?' Clare teased, relaxed as they drank their coffee.

Rena spluttered with laughter. 'I was hoping you wouldn't remember that.'

'Why?'

'I married him!'

'Rena!' Clare laughed, a low husky sound that had several male heads turning in their direction, obviously appreciatively. 'Did you really?' she asked once she had sobered.

'Mm,' Rena nodded. 'I got tired of running.'

'And?'

Her friend gave a rueful shrug. 'I love him too much to describe how happy I am, how happy being with him makes me. But then I don't need to explain that to you, do I?'

Didn't she? The sadness returned to her golden eyes, the cool hauteur back. She was fond of Harvey, knew that he was equally fond of her, that they would have a good marriage, but they certainly didn't have the nerve-shattering ecstasy Rena meant. They were comfortable together, shared the same interests, but their lovemaking never gave her such intense pleasure that the rest of the world ceased to exist.

But no, Rena didn't have to describe those feelings to her. She knew about them, she just didn't have them with Harvey.

'Do you have any children?' she asked now.

'Not yet,' Rena grinned. 'Maybe soon, although we aren't in any hurry.'

'Where is Alan now?'

Her friend pulled a face. 'In England,' she sighed. 'He's a lawyer, a busy one. It gets harder and harder to accept these parts that take me away from him.'

'Then don't,' Clare said simply.

'It's this business, it gets into your blood,' Rena dismissed. 'One day I'll know it's time to stop, but I'm not
quite ready yet.'

'Talking of business,' Clare looked pointedly at her
wrist-watch, 'I'd better go and tidy up for this meeting
this afternoon. Jason doesn't like unpunctuality.'

'Jason?' the other girl frowned.

'Our director, dear,' she teased.

'Oh, but he isn't,' Rena shook her head. 'At least, he
wasn't the last I heard.'

Clare frowned her puzzlement. 'And what did you
hear?'

She shrugged. 'That Faulkner had an accident of
some sort, I'm not sure what. They were looking around
for another director.'

'Did they find one?'

'Well, we're here, aren't we?' Rena grinned.

'I suppose so,' Clare agreed slowly.

'I would have thought they would have told you.'

So would she, which meant she had to talk to Harvey.
'I'm just going back to my room. I'll see you later.'

'Sure.' Rena stood up, giving a casual wave.

Clare hurried back to Harvey's room, getting lost a
couple of times and having to ask the way, being further
delayed as the people she asked recognised her and
asked for her autograph.

The feelings of apprehension she had been experienc-
ing since she had accepted the part of Caroline suddenly
seemed to loom up black and dangerous. She should
never have agreed to come here, should have followed
her instinct and stayed far away from Los Angeles.

Harvey took some time to answer the door, and she
tapped her shoe impatiently on the floor as she waited.
He looked less than his usual immaculate self when he
at last opened the door, a robe pulled hastily over his
nakedness, his fair hair tousled from sleep.

But Clare cared nothing for this, walking agitatedly
into the room and closing the door behind her.

Harvey blinked to clear the sleep from his head. 'What's the matter? Shouldn't you be on your way to the meeting?'

Her mouth twisted. 'The meeting Jason called—only it wasn't Jason, was it?' Her tone was brittle.

'Oh lord!' He put a hand to his temple. 'With the rush of the last few days I forgot to tell you——'

'Tell me now, Harvey,' she encouraged sharply.

'Faulkner had an accident a week or so ago, a fall from a horse, I think. He broke his leg.'

'So he's completely out of the picture?' Clare said with dread.

'Afraid so,' her fiancé nodded.

'But I—Who's replacing him?' she demanded abruptly.

'Didn't I tell you?' he frowned. 'No, I don't suppose I did. Well, it obviously had to be someone who could act as well as direct——'

'Yes?' she prompted tensely.

'They managed to get Rourke Somerville,' Harvey told her excitedly. 'A piece of luck really. Normally he wouldn't have been free, but the film he should have been working on has been delayed several months. I think he . . .'

Harvey's voice continued to drone on, but Clare was no longer listening. Rourke . . . Oh God, Rourke was here, on this very ship, and she was going to be working with him!

CHAPTER TWO

'CLARE!' Harvey was frowning at her.

She blinked dazedly. 'Yes?'

'I was talking to you,' his tone was petulant, 'and you haven't heard a word I said.'

'You were saying how lucky we were to get Rourke Somerville,' she recalled dully.

'Yes,' he acknowledged eagerly. 'If anything he's better than Jason Faulkner.'

Clare was regaining her composure now, forcing herself to mentally collect herself together. 'Do you think so?' she said in a bored voice, once again the 'Ice Lady' one perceptive newspaper had nicknamed her. The name had mainly been chosen out of pique by the reporter when she had refused his invitation to dinner, but nevertheless it was a truer description than 'Golden Lady'.

'Of course.' Harvey seemed not to have noticed her withdrawn attitude, that momentary slip of composure. Which was perhaps as well, because she had no intention of explaining the reason for it to him! 'If anything Rourke Somerville is a bigger box-office draw then you are.'

Clare gave a mocking smile. 'Is that a good thing? As my manager aren't you supposed to get me top billing?'

'Oh, you'll get that,' Harvey took her seriously. 'Somerville has no objection to your taking top billing over him. After all, his name will be under director too.'

Yes. And Rourke had had a sight longer than she had to become accustomed to the fact that they were to star in this film together, were to act as *lovers*. God, he must find the situation funny! If Rena hadn't casually mentioned the change of director to her she would have

24

walked into that meeting this afternoon totally un-
prepared. As it was she was going to find it difficult, if
not impossible, to do.

'Clare!' Harvey gave her an impatient frown for her
lack of attention. 'Maybe I should call and tell them
you can't make the meeting,' he frowned. 'You seem to
be suffering from jet-lag.'

She longed to accept the reprieve offered to her, and
yet she couldn't do it. Rourke was sure to know the real
reason, and she wouldn't give him the satisfaction of
thinking she was frightened of meeting him again—even
if it were true!

It was five years since she had last seen him, five years
when she had tried not to even think about him, five
years during which she had matured into a self-confident
woman who wouldn't allow a rake like him to get to
her. He couldn't touch her, not now or in the past; she
had Harvey now, and would one day be his wife. Then
why was she filled with such alarm just as the prospect
of seeing Rourke again . . .?

She straightened her shoulders determinedly. 'That
won't be necessary, Harvey,' she said coolly. 'I feel perfectly well enough to attend this—meeting.' The nervous
fluttering in her stomach wouldn't be stilled. 'I have to
go now,' she told him jerkily. 'I don't want to be late.'

'Okay, darling,' he kissed her tenderly on the mouth.
'And if you would rather have dinner in your room
tonight that's fine by me.'

'Thank you, Harvey,' she said, touched by his gentleness. 'Perhaps you would like to join me?' she offered
generously.

His handsome face became flushed with desire.
'Clare . . .!' he murmured huskily, his lips claiming hers
in a kiss that told her of his passion.

Harvey desired her, she had always known that. And
after accepting his ring she had allowed him more inti-
macies with her body, feeling his hand on her breast
now, and yet so far they had never completely made

love. Maybe if they had she would be able to banish rakishly attractive untidy black hair and twinkling blue eyes from her mind. Maybe from her body too . . .

She extricated herself from Harvey's arms with a consoling smile. 'I have to go. I'll see you later.'

He was breathing raggedly, his eyes bright with suppressed desire. 'I'll look forward to it,' he told her throatily.

Clare left with a quick, warm smile, but the smile faded as soon as she closed the door behind her. Twenty to two—she didn't have to go to the Windsor Room quite yet, so she hurried back to her suite, shutting herself in with a feeling of relief.

Rourke Somerville! God, Rourke . . . She collapsed into one of the comfortable armchairs, closing her eyes to shut out the pain just hearing his name again had caused. In her mind she could see it all, all the pain, the disillusionment that she had thought forgotten, or at least buried. But it was far from being that, the memories, all of them, as vivid as if it had all happened yesterday.

She was eighteen again, newly arrived from England, having left school to come home and consider what she was going to do with the rest of her life.

Charles, her mother's chauffeur, had met her at the airport as usual, her girlish pleasure as she climbed into the limousine still as delighted as the first time she had come home from school and been met in this way. She had been coming to Los Angeles for holidays for the past ten years, but this time it was different, this time she didn't have to go back to England if she didn't want to.

The house in Beverly Hills had seemed as spectacular as usual, the pink and white painted hacienda-style house at the end of the long tree-edged driveway. Her mother had lived in this house for the last fifteen years, much acclaimed by the film world, often not even at home when Clare got there, more often than not on location in some exotic part of the world working on her latest film.

But she was home today, resting after a gruelling year filming the movie that was taking the world by storm.

Laughter could be heard coming from the direction of the pool as Clare stepped out of the car, both male and female.

'Your mother had guests for lunch,' Charles informed her in a deadpan voice. An import from England, he had been with her mother for the last twenty years, his trust and loyalty to his employer never in any doubt.

Clare had often wondered whether he and her mother had once been lovers, for Charles' devotion to her mother was almost dog-like, despite her often volatile temper.

Clare had never known her father; he had apparently been killed in an automobile accident just after she was born. He had been an actor too, as famous as her mother was now, and with two such talented parents she was seriously considering an acting career for herself.

'Thank you, Charles,' she smiled as he carried her suitcase into her bedroom, moving forward to the balcony once he had left the room. There were about a dozen people sitting around the pool, but only one person actually in the water.

Her mother was draped decorously on one of the loungers. She was already forty years of age, despite her claim of being thirty. She was wearing a black bikini, two scraps of material that were only just decent, so it was no wonder she didn't want to get it wet. It would probably dissove in the water! Her beautiful face was partly obscured by huge, round sunglasses, but Clare knew her eyes were deeply brown beneath them, her skin clear and youthful. Her hair was a deep auburn, thick and naturally straight to just below her shoulders, although having seen photographs of her mother as a child Clare knew it was kept that rich red colour by artificial means; her hair was really a mousy brown.

She considered her mother the most beautiful woman she had ever seen, magnetically so, and she could see the men in the party were all in love with that beauty. All except the man in the pool . . .

She looked at him with interest, mainly because he wasn't one of the men who paid court to her mother. He was swimming the length of the pool with long, easy strokes, black hair plastered over his forehead, worn longer than was fashionable at the moment, although he didn't look as if fashion particularly bothered him.

As he swung out of the pool Clare gasped her recognition. Rourke Somerville! He was the man starring with her mother in her latest film, the one everyone was raving about at the moment. One of her friends at school had a poster of him on her bedroom wall, and at the time Clare had thought the picture flattered the actor; now she knew that if anything it understated.

Rourke Somerville had the physique of an athlete, was tall, extremely so, with wide powerful shoulders, a slim waist, and muscular thighs, his only clothing a pair of black swimming trunks, and by the look of his tan he didn't always wear them! His legs were long and firmly muscled, the whole of his body covered lightly with black hair.

As if sensing her scrutiny he suddenly looked up at the balcony she stood on, and Clare quickly ducked back into the room, but not before she had taken in every devastating feature. He had towelled his hair dry on stepping out of the pool, and it now hung in damp waves about his face, as black as night. His brows were the same dark colour, jutting over the deepest blue eyes Clare had ever seen, his lashes long and thick. His nose was long and straight, arrogantly so, his mouth full-lipped, the lower lip sensually so, his jaw square and determined, giving the impression of a haughty disregard for anyone's wishes but his own. A gold medallion hung about the wide column of his throat, suspended there by a thick, chunky gold chain; even the single piece of jewellery he wore was totally masculine.

She wanted to go down and join them, to perhaps talk to Rourke Somerville. How jealous Diana would be when she wrote and told her about it! Her friend knew everything about him, his Irish-American parentage, his upbringing in an orphanage until he was sixteen years old, the way he had worked his way up to the top of his profession, until now, at the age of thirty-four, he could pick and choose the parts he played for any fee he demanded.

In one of the infrequent letters Clare had received from her mother she had been full of praise for her co-star. And it seemed they were still friends, otherwise he wouldn't have been invited here. She wondered what Perry, her mother's boy-friend for the last year, would think of that.

She was in the process of putting on her bikini when the door opened. Already wearing the yellow briefs that matched the top, she had paused to study her body in the full-length mirror before putting on the bra-top. Her breasts were full and pert, the tips rosy peaks, her waist flat and slender, her hips and thighs reed-thin. Until this last year she had had puppy-fat to contend with, and added to her height she had felt like an elephant. Fortunately she had slimmed down, and might even have considered a career in modelling if it weren't for her full breasts.

To the man now standing in the doorway she must have looked as if she were blatantly admiring herself. She snatched up the bra of her bikini, clutching it in front of her as she stared at Rourke Somerville in fascinated horror.

His gaze was frankly appraising as he came farther into the room, closing the door behind him, still wearing only the brief black trunks. 'I thought I hadn't imagined you,' he murmured, his voice having a magical lilt to it that charmed without effort. 'Where have you been hiding yourself?' he asked huskily.

'I—Why, nowhere.' But she wished she could hide herself now, knowing this man had taken in every naked inch of her—and by the glint in his eyes he had liked what he saw!

He walked slowly over to where she was, unsuccessfully, trying to hide herself, plucking the bikini top out of her nervous fingers, holding her hands down at her sides as he slowly looked at her. The eyes he finally raised to hers had flickering flames lighting their deep blue depths. 'I've certainly never met you before,' he said throatily.

Clare licked her lips, not realising how provocative the movement was. 'You haven't?' she delayed, her embarrassment fading, and a languorous warmth starting to invade her lower limbs under his avid gaze, her eyes the colour of rich, molten gold.

Rourke Somerville smiled, his teeth very white against his tanned skin. 'I would have remembered you,' he murmured, releasing her hands to run his fingertips lightly over the flatness of her stomach, a devil entering his eyes as his hands came to rest at the top of her bikini briefs. He laughed softly in his throat as he heard her catch her breath, those sensuous hands moving up towards her breasts now, his gaze fixed firmly on her flushed face, smiling as he watched her reaction to his caresses.

She flinched as he touched her breasts. Ten years of convent education had not prepared her for the sensuality of this man. The nearest the nuns had ever come to discussing sex had been in the Biology class, and then it had only been mentioned briefly as part of life's cycle.

But this man was everything the nuns had ever warned her about in a man—and everything the other girls had ever whispered about in their secret fantasies!

'Please don't do that!' She shuddered as his hands resumed their exploration of her lower body.

He raised heavy lids. 'Why not?'

'Because—well, because——'

He shook his head. 'But I want to touch you. You're like sunshine, do you know that?' One of his hands moved to cup her chin, rubbing his thumb caressingly over her lips. 'Young, fresh, and bright.'

'Please——'

'No need to ask, Sunshine,' he said huskily, his head bending towards hers. 'I have no intention of leaving this room until I've at least kissed you.'

Dating boys hadn't exactly been encouraged at the convent, although Clare had had her fair share of dates. But they had been with boys, boys of her own age, and Rourke Somerville was definitely a man, in every sense of the word.

As his mouth moved druggingly over hers he pulled her thighs in between his, their bathing suits no barrier to the throb of Rourke's body, and her lips parted willingly beneath his.

His hands moved beneath her bikini to cup her heated flesh, moving his thighs against her as he held her steady, leaving her in no doubt of his full arousal.

Clare panicked. Everything was moving too fast for her inexperience, and she wrenched her mouth away from his, pushing at his hands. 'Please—stop!' She looked at him with darkened eyes. 'Stop . . .' she groaned as his lips moved to the sensitive cord in her throat.

'You don't really want me to do that,' he taunted softly. 'And I don't want to either.'

'But I do!' she cried, finally managing to push him away, her breathing heavy as she escaped his arms. Rourke watched the heaving of her breasts until she snatched up the blouse she had worn for the flight, pulling it on over her nakedness.

Rourke shrugged, making no effort to hide the arousal of his own body. 'What's the panic?' he shrugged.

She gave him an angry glare. 'The panic is that you shouldn't be in here.' And he certainly shouldn't have touched her the way he had! Her skin still tingled from the contact.

'Why?'

'Because—You just shouldn't!' she said angrily, knowing that while she might tell Diana she had met Rourke Somerville, she would never tell her what else had happened between them.

His eyebrows rose. 'You aren't the maid or something, are you?'

'Of course not!' She flushed.

'Of course not.' He looked pointedly around the luxurious bedroom she was occupying, the totally feminine lemon and white decor. 'Darling, anyone who comes to one of Carlene's parties knows the score,' he drawled.

Clare blinked hard. 'They—they do?'

'Mm,' he nodded. 'Anything goes—and I mean anything. So if we choose to spend the rest of the afternoon in bed together no one is going to mind.'

'No!' She backed away as he advanced, more shocked by what he was saying than she wanted him to know. Did her mother really give parties like *that*?

'Why not?' His deep blue eyes narrowed. 'Or is one of those guys downstairs yours'?'

'Guys? Downstairs . . .? Oh no,' she realised he meant the other men by the pool. 'No,' she shook her head firmly.

'Then what's wrong?' His mouth twisted. 'Don't tell me you don't like me!'

She knew she deserved his mockery. Of course she couldn't deny liking him, she hadn't exactly screamed the place down when he had kissed and caressed her. And this man was too experienced with women not to know she had responded totally to him.

'No . . .' she acknowledged faintly.

'And I certainly like you. Relax, beautiful,' he grinned, his hands lightly grasping the tops of her arms to pull her slowly towards him. 'If you want to take it slow we'll take it slow,' he shrugged. 'But not here. Let's go back to my place, relax—you can even sunbathe nude if you want to,' he added throatily. 'I often do.'

He was only confirming what she had already guessed, and the transition from the convent to nude sunbathing was too much of a shock for her to do anything else but blush.

Rourke's eyes narrowed on her fiery cheeks. 'Who are you?' he asked in a puzzled voice, his hands dropping away from her arms.

'I——'

'Rourke? Rourke, where are you?'

His mouth twisted as he half turned towards the door. 'Our beautiful hostess,' he drawled. 'Which means I'd better get out of here.'

'Yes,' Clare agreed, her eyes wide, terrified her mother was going to come in here and find her in a state of undress with Rourke Somerville. He might claim that her mother gave wild parties, but she had never seen any evidence of them; her mother was very strict about her behaviour whenever she was at home.

Rourke shrugged. 'Maybe the daughter's arrived from the convent. You have her to thank for not being able to show us all that beautiful body of yours.'

She gulped. 'I—I do?'

He nodded. 'Mm. Carlene ordered bathing suits to be worn in her daughter's honour.'

Did that mean they usually bathed nude...? Including her mother? No, she couldn't believe that. And this man obviously didn't realise that she was 'the daughter' who was spoiling all his fun.

'You'd better go,' she advised softly.

'Yes,' he sighed, looking impatient. 'Are you coming down to join us?'

'I—In a minute.' When she had recovered from the shock of the last fifteen minutes!

He strolled casually over to the door, tall and lithe, moving with an animal grace that was totally sensual.

'I'll be waiting for you,' he said softly. 'And don't forget the rest of your bikini—we wouldn't want to shock the child.'

Clare's mouth compressed in consternation as Rourke Somerville left the room. How old did he think she was, for goodness' sake!

Her sense of humour got the better of her, and she giggled at the idea of the little girl he expected her to be. How surprised he was going to be when he found out he had just been making love to 'the child'!

But it wasn't really funny, and she sobered instantly. Rourke Somerville had touched her intimately, hadn't expected her to be surprised by his behaviour. Just what sort of man was he? And what sort of girl did he think she was!

She had all her bikini on when her mother entered the room a few minutes later, running to meet her with a tiny sob. She hadn't seen her mother for almost a year because she had been busy filming, and yet she found her little changed, her beauty as youthful as ever.

'Mummy!' She hugged her, feeling ridiculously tearful.

'Hello, darling,' her mother greeted in her offhand voice. 'Don't cling, Clare, it's much too hot for body contact.' She stepped away from Clare, her sunglasses now pushed back into her hair.

Her mother's words reminded her of the body contact she had just had with Rourke Somerville, and she felt suddenly shy. 'You're looking well, Mummy,' she said awkwardly, feeling tall and gauche against her mother's petite beauty and grace.

'Thank you, darling.' Carlene looked pleased by the compliment. 'And so are you,' she frowned, tiny lines appearing at the sides of her eyes. 'When did you grow to be so—attractive?'

Clare gave a happy laugh, flushing her pleasure. 'I've slimmed down, that's all.'

'No, that isn't all!' Her mother's voice was sharp. 'Oh

well, never mind,' she dismissed irritably. 'Gene's waiting for you downstairs.'

Clare's face lit up with excitement. Gene was Perry's son, and the two of them had dated casually the last time she was home. It would be lovely to see him again.

'I don't suppose you've seen—No,' her mother answered her own question, 'I don't suppose you have. Come along, Clare, I can't neglect my guests any longer.'

The two of them walked down the stairs together, totally different to look at, both startlingly beautiful, although Clare would never have guessed that her own youthful beauty far outshone that of her mother. In her opinion no one could be as beautiful as her mother. All her life she had been in awe of that beauty, and now was no different.

'Seen who, Mummy?' she asked casually.

'What?' Her mother seemed preoccupied. 'Oh, one of the guests seems to have wandered off. I didn't know if you'd seen him.'

So she was still looking for Rourke. Maybe he had left; he seemed to have been bored by the party. But he had said he would be waiting for her, and somehow she believed he would be.

The two women stepped into the pool area together, one with hair like sunshine, her youthful perfection giving her a feline grace, the other with hair like flame, a woman conscious that her own beauty was beginning to fade—and determined to hang on to it, and the power it gave her, at all costs.

'Hello . . .'

Clare instantly recognised that husky purr, and turned apprehensive eyes on Rourke Somerville. He had a drink in his hand now, a long, slim glass that contained some form of alcohol, she felt sure. And his hair was completely dry now, loose black curls that lay in complete disorder across his brow, giving him a rakish attraction that made her pulses race.

'Ah, there you are, Rourke.' It was her mother who

answered him, slipping her arm into the crook of his. 'I
thought you'd gone, darling,' she added throatily, looking very small and feminine against his broad masculinity.

He looked down at her with amused indulgence. 'And
miss meeting your beautiful guest?' His deep blue gaze
caught and held Clare's gold one, and her breathing
was suddenly constricted.

Her mother frowned, her normally smooth brow
creased into lines of puzzlement. 'Guest? What
guest——? Oh, you mean Clare,' she snapped her irritation.

Rourke ignored her, his gaze slowly caressing Clare,
his mouth curved into an intimate smile, as if they
shared a secret.

She blushed scarlet, knowing that because of her behaviour with him earlier he had a right to look at her in
that—*knowing* way.

'If that's her name, yes,' he answered her mother but
continued to look at her, his gaze on her mouth almost
a caress.

'Well, it is,' her mother's voice was sharp. 'And she
isn't a guest.'

His eyes narrowed, his expression wary now. 'She
isn't?' he asked slowly.

'Of course not. This is my daughter,' he was informed
almost angrily.

Her mother had all of his attention now; all the lazy
sensuality disappeared as he looked from one to the
other of them, apparently trying to see some sign of
likeness between them. Clare knew he would find none.
She took after her father, Drew Anderson, both of them
being tall and fair. Even her features were nothing like
her mother's, her mother having an almost elfin beauty,
while her own features were more regular and rounded.

Now he frowned. 'This is "little Clare"?' he derided.

Her mother flushed. 'Yes.'

His mouth twisted. 'She's hardly little, Carlene.'

Her mother's laugh sounded forced. 'She is rather tall——'

'I wasn't talking about her height,' Rourke drawled, his gaze frankly admiring on Clare's curves.

'Really, Rourke,' her mother's voice was brittlely light now, 'you can't flirt with my daughter!'

His mouth tightened grimly, his eyes becoming hard. 'No, I can't,' he agreed tautly, extricating himself from her hand. 'I have to go now, Carlene——'

'Oh, not yet, Rourke,' she pouted provocatively. 'Stay to dinner, everyone else is.'

'It isn't possible,' he refused smoothly. 'I have another appointment this evening.'

Clare's eyes widened; she knew this statement to be untrue. He had invited her to spend the evening with him, so he certainly didn't have another appointment. He looked at her in challenge, as if daring her to dispute his claim, but she remained silent.

'Oh, Rourke,' her mother chided disappointedly.

'Oh, Carlene!' he taunted.

'Tomorrow, then?' her mother insisted.

'We'll see.' He was noncommittal. 'Miss Walters,' he nodded in Clare's direction, already turning to go and change when she corrected him.

'Anderson,' she said huskily.

Blue eyes swung back in her direction. 'I beg your pardon?' he drawled.

She drew herself up to her full height, still only on a level with his nose. 'My name is Anderson, Mr Somerville,' she told him coolly. 'Clare Anderson.'

'I see,' he mocked. 'I'll remember that for future reference.'

'I doubt we'll meet again,' she snapped, unable to stop herself. Heavens, he was so arrogant! How dared he treat her mother so casually!

His eyes narrowed as he sensed her resentment. 'Oh, I think we will, Clare. In fact, I'm sure of it.'

She felt relieved when he at last moved towards the

house to change, and turned gratefully as someone
called her name.

'Gene!' she smiled recognition of the tall sun-bronzed
boy standing in front of her. He hadn't changed at
all, was still as good-looking as ever, his blond hair
sun-bleached, his eyes a deep attractive brown, wearing
only a pair of cut-off denims, his body lean and sun-
tanned.

'Hello, beautiful!' He didn't stand on ceremony, but
picked her up to swing her round, kissing her soundly
on the mouth.

After being with Gene for ten minutes it was as if she
had never been away; the two of them were once again
enjoying each other's company. Perry smiled at them
indulgently; a man in his mid-forties, very handsome,
with prematurely iron-grey hair, liking the fact that his
son and the daughter of the woman he loved liked each
other.

'Rourke's leaving, darling,' her mother called Perry
over to them.

Clare couldn't resist looking at Rourke Somerville
once more, to find him looking at her too, a lazily
amused smile curving his lips. She hurriedly looked
away again, but not before she had noticed everything
about him, his hair a riot of black curls, a deep blue silk
shirt fitting snugly across his chest and flat stomach,
tucked into the low waistband of his white trousers. He
held a pair of sunglasses in his hand as he talked to her
mother and Perry, even such a simple movement looking
sensual on this man.

With a mocking nod in her direction he was gone—
and with him went all the fun and gaiety of the party,
or so it seemed to Clare.

The next few days were spent mainly in Gene's company, their days being spent at Malibu Beach, where
Gene spent most of his time on his surfboard, although
the waves hardly seemed high enough to accommodate
him. But he enjoyed it, and Clare found it relaxing to be

in his company. Their evenings were spent going to one party after another, renewing old acquaintances for Clare, and often making new ones. It was at one of these parties that she met Rourke for the second time.

She hadn't completely forgotten him, but she had pushed the thought of him to the back of her mind. He hadn't been to the house any more, and her mother never mentioned him, so it was hard to find out anything about him. Not that she was altogether sure she wanted to find out anything about such a dangerous man; just remembering the way he had looked at her sending shivers of apprehension down her spine. And his words that they would meet again had sounded almost like a threat to her sensitive ears.

It was almost a week later that Gene and she were at yet another party, the only thing making this one different from the others being that Rourke Somerville had arrived shortly after eleven o'clock, a beautiful blonde on his arm, a woman that Clare instantly recognised as Livia Marriott, an actress known for her more 'revealing' roles. The last film she had made had been banned in many parts of the world, and it seemed she was no less daring in her private life, the black dress she almost had on having no back at all and hardly any front.

Rourke was dressed almost as casually, his white trousers skin-tight, his black shirt almost completely unbuttoned, the hair visible on his chest thick and dark.

Clare tried not to notice him and his affectionate partner, but it was impossible not to. When they danced together they almost made love, and when they didn't dance Livia Marriott draped herself so sensuously over Rourke that they might as well have been making love then too.

She looked away, shocked by their behaviour, although no one else seemed to be taking the least bit of notice. Some of the other women in the room even looked jealous of the full-breasted actress—probably wishing themselves in her place, Clare thought disgustedly.

'Why the frown?'

Once again Rourke had caught her unawares, leaning casually against the wall as she sat in a corner waiting for Gene to return from dancing with one of their friends.

She blushed. 'I didn't see you, Mr Somerville,' she said stiltedly.

He moved to sit on the side of her armchair, much too close for comfort, smelling of some spicy, masculine cologne. 'So the frown wasn't for me?' he asked throatily.

Clare moved uncomfortably, sure that he must be able to see straight down the low neckline of her cream halter-necked dress. And the frown had been for him, for his blatant behaviour with the young actress. 'I didn't say that, Mr Somerville,' she told him stiffly, her years at the convent preventing her telling a deliberate lie.

'Oh?' His eyebrows rose. 'What did I do this time?'

'This time?' She blinked her puzzlement, licking her lips nervously.

Rourke watched the movement, and those flames started to leap in his eyes once again. 'Do you do that on purpose?' he rasped.

Clare frowned. 'Do what?'

He gave her a disbelieving look, his mouth twisting derisively. 'Never mind,' he dismissed scathingly. 'So, what did I do?'

'I—Why, nothing.' She went to stand up, totally unnerved by his closeness, but Rourke's hand on her arm stopped her. 'Let me go,' she requested softly.

'Why?'

'Why . . .?'

'Yes. You know you don't want me to really,' his eyes teased her. 'You aren't what I expected "little Clare" to look like. Not at all,' he added mockingly.

She already knew that! 'What *did* you expect, Mr

Somerville, white socks and a gymslip?' she flashed, resenting the hold on her arm that wouldn't be shaken.

His mouth quirked into a smile. 'Now there's a thought,' he leered wickedly.

Clare tried to be annoyed, but her humour got the better of her as she burst out laughing. 'The nuns would be shocked,' she giggled.

Rourke's eyes darkened appreciatively. 'I'm sure they would.' He stood up in one fluid movement. 'Let's dance,' he said abruptly.

'Oh, but I—Miss Marriott?'

He smiled. 'So *that's* what I did wrong. Livia is busy—seducing a director.'

Clare's eyes widened. 'Don't you mind?'

'Should I?' He sounded bored.

'Well, I—You came here together!'

'So?'

'So you—well, you——'

He shrugged. 'Livia and I make no claims on each other. Does Gene have any claim on you?' His eyes were narrowed.

'Gene . . .?' she repeated in bewilderment.

'The beautiful young daughter of Carlene Walters and the son of Perry Lester have been seen together all over L.A., at the beach, at restaurants, at parties,' he added pointedly. 'Didn't you know you're the talk of the town?'

'No,' her face was scarlet with embarrassment. 'Gene and I are just friends——'

Rourke gave a mocking laugh. 'Now where have I heard that before?' he taunted.

Clare blushed. 'I don't think you're a very nice person, Mr Somerville.'

'I hope not,' he still smiled.

'You're impossible!' She spluttered with laughter, finding this outrageous man more and more attractive by the minute.

'I hope I'm that too,' he nodded. 'Now, shall we dance?'

'Yes, please,' she accepted shyly.

'I thought you were never going to agree,' he groaned, taking her to the dance area before pulling her unresistingly into his arms.

Not an inch separated them as they slowly danced to the music, Clare resting her head on Rourke's shoulder, her arms about his neck as his hands rested possessively on her hips.

'Now aren't you glad you didn't become a nun?' he murmured in amusement, his lips warm against her earlobe.

Clare smiled. 'There was never any chance of that.' She respected the wishes of the Sisters to shut themselves away from the world, from the love of a flesh-and-blood man, but she knew it wasn't for her. She enjoyed being kissed, being held, and she knew that one day she wanted a husband and children to take care of.

'No,' Rourke gave a throaty chuckle, one of his hands exploring the curve of her spine now. 'No, I don't suppose there was.'

For some reason she didn't like the way he said that, and she stiffened in his arms before moving away from him. 'I think I'd like to return to Gene now,' she said stiltedly.

Blue eyes narrowed with displeasure, his lashes ridiculously long for a man. 'And if I don't want you to?'

Her brows rose with more calm than she was feeling. 'Should it matter to me what you want?'

She was surprised at her own coolness, her pulse fluttering erratically just to look at him. But she had seen the way her mother handled men, and she knew that if she showed Rourke how nervous he really made her feel he would tease her unmercifully—worse, he would know how deeply she was attracted to him.

And she was attracted, very much so. She had known it the moment she saw him again; a nervous fluttering was beginning in the pit of her stomach, an excited flush coming to her cheeks. And she could quite cheerfully have scratched Livia Marriott's eyes out for the way she kept touching him, pressing herself against him while he looked on in amusement.

It was that amusement that attracted too, the challenge his contemptuous attitude towards women gave every female who so much as looked at him. And he was contemptuous. He found women amusing, playthings, and to her shame Clare knew that she would like to act just as clinging as the other women in his life. But she wouldn't. She might only be eighteen, lack the experience to control a man like this, but she was sensible enough to know that Rourke Somerville enjoyed the chase more than the capture. With a maturity beyond her years she knew that he was intrigued by her, that he found the contradictions of her sun-kissed appearance and her convent upbringing a challenge he had never faced before.

'It matters to me what you want,' he answered her now. 'Do you want me?'

His direct approach was too much for her, and she blushed a deep red. 'Certainly not!' she replied in a shocked voice.

'I want you.'

Clare swallowed hard. 'You—you do?'

'Mm,' he nodded, his eyes warm on her lips. 'When can I have you?'

'You can't!' She moved completely away from him. 'Excuse me, Mr Somerville, I have to get back to Gene.'

He shrugged philosophically, letting her go without a word of protest. Clare couldn't decide whether she was piqued or relieved at his easy acceptance of her departure from his side. In the end she decided she was piqued. She hadn't been so clever after all; Rourke regarded her with just as much amusement as he did every other woman he came into contact with.

She found Gene out by the pool, and her eyes widened

as she saw there were several people in the water—all of them completely naked, male and female alike!

Gene put his arm protectively about her shoulders. 'Time to leave, I think,' he grinned.

'I'm not a prude, you know,' she snapped, still raw from Rourke's casual treatment.

'Hey, I know that,' Gene chided. 'But it's getting late. And I make it a rule never to get involved in this sort of scene. It can only get worse,' he grimaced. 'Let's leave.'

Clare was secretly relieved by his decision, although she remained outwardly calm, waiting in the spacious hallway while Gene went in search of her jacket.

'Leaving already?' remarked an all too familiar voice.

Her hands clenched at her sides, but she faced Rourke coolly enough, tall and beautiful, the cream colour of her dress giving her skin a golden glow, her hair like burnished gold as it hung straight to her shoulders, the fringe winged back over her tawny eyes.

They were strangely alone out here, as the rest of the party were in the spacious lounge and pool area. Rourke looked dark and disturbing—mainly disturbing, all amusement gone now as he continued to look at her, his eyes a deep, dark blue.

'The fun's just beginning,' he added in a murmur, standing perhaps six feet away from her, his masculinity a tangible thing.

Clare's mouth twisted derisively. 'It depends on what you call fun,' she drawled, pleased with herself as she managed to infuse just the right amount of contempt into her voice.

One dark eyebrow rose, and Rourke moved several steps forward, standing only inches away from her now. 'And what's your idea of fun, Clare?' he asked huskily.

She maintained a calm exterior with effort, inside her emotions in complete turmoil. No man had the right to have so much animal magnetism, not and be allowed loose among the susceptible female population—of which she was one.

She felt sure he would be riveting on the big screen. She had never personally seen any of his films, but Diana had seen every one several times, exclaiming over the sexuality he brought into the roles he played.

'Certainly not what's going on in there,' she nodded in the direction of the pool.

'No?'

'No,' she blushed. 'I prefer a—a one-on-one basis,' she added bravely.

'So do I.' He took another step forward, fitting his body against hers, each hard contour evident against her softer curves. 'Do you have to go?' he asked throatily.

'I—Yes.' Excited colour heightened her cheeks, a fevered look to her eyes. Gene often kissed her, touched her in a casual way—but there was nothing casual about Rourke's touch, and heat coursed through her body as she began to tremble.

'Do you really?' he said huskily, slowly bending his head to claim her mouth for the second time since she had known him.

It was just as nerve-shattering as before, the slow, drugging movement of his lips on hers, the erotic way he ran his hands over her bare back, her flesh seeming to tingle where he touched.

'Stay, Clare,' he breathed against her mouth.

'I——'

'Stay!' he urged, his mouth more urgent this time, telling her better than words of his desire for her. 'Or better still,' he raised his head to groan, 'come home with me.'

The warning bells began ringing more strongly where this man was concerned, and she reluctantly pulled away from him. A look of angry irritation flitted across his hard face before it was quickly masked by his usual look of cynicism, telling her that it was a long time since any woman had turned him down.

'Unfortunately,' she drawled confidently, 'you aren't

the man I want to be one-on-one with.'

Anger blazed in the deep blue eyes before it was quickly controlled. 'Are you telling me Gene Lester is?' he mocked insultingly.

She raised her brows in cool query, sure that she had a vocation for acting—if this performance were anything to go by? Rourke was completely taken in by her blasé attitude. 'Is there any reason why he shouldn't be?' she asked distantly.

Rourke scowled. 'He's too damned young for you!'

'He happens to be twenty.'

His mouth twisted. 'And you're eighteen going on thirty-five!'

He was being deliberately insulting, she knew that, but was that really how she appeared to him? He made it sound as if she were too experienced for Gene. She might have responded to Rourke's kisses, but she didn't think that was any basis on which to make such an assumption about her.

'Clare!' Gene, luckily, arrived at her side at that moment, placing her lightweight jacket about her bare shoulders. 'How are you, Rourke?' he greeted the other man with his usual friendly manner.

'Fine,' the other man answered tersely. 'I think I'll get back to the party.'

Clare knew this last was added for her benefit, making her wonder if he were about to join in the nude bathing. Livia Marriott had already been in the pool! An angry sparkle lit up her eyes. Well, let him! Why should she care? And no doubt the beautiful actress, or one of the other women here, would be sharing his bed later tonight. No matter how she denied it that gave her a painful wrench in her chest.

'I'd stay away from him if I were you,' Gene remarked on the drive back to her home.

She looked at him with startled eyes. 'Sorry?'

'Rourke Somerville is bad news for any girl, but especially you.'

Clare frowned. 'Why especially me?' she snapped.

Gene gave her a sideways glance, smiling. 'You're such an innocent——'

'That could change!' she said resentfully.

He gave her a sharp look, serious now. 'Not with Rourke Somerville?'

'Why not?'

'Clare!'

'Well, why not?' she repeated irritably.

He gave an angry sigh, shaking his head. 'If you don't know I'm not going to tell you.'

Maybe he should have told her; if he had she would probably have been spared a lot of pain. But Gene hadn't proffered any information, and she had been too angry to ask him, sure that he was only acting that way because he believed her incapable of having a man like Rourke Somerville interested in her.

Oh, the conceit of youth! Gene had known very well that Rourke had her picked out as his next victim—and he also knew what it was going to do to her. Despite his happy-go-lucky attitude Gene had seen exactly what was going to happen, and——

'I realise you're the star of this movie, Miss Anderson,' an icy voice interrupted her memories, a voice that was so familiar she instantly paled. 'But when I call a meeting of the whole cast I damn well expect the *whole* cast to be there—and that includes you, lady,' the last was said aggressively.

Clare turned stricken eyes towards the open door, swallowing hard as she saw Rourke standing there, the man who had been her lover five years ago.

CHAPTER THREE

HE hadn't changed at all, despite being thirty-nine now. He still wore his hair longer than was fashionable, still had a lean, muscular body, shown to advantage now in cream trousers and a dark green shirt. And he was still as handsome as ever, breathtakingly so.

Only his eyes had changed—or maybe that was because he was so furiously angry with her. A devil no longer glinted in their depths, no light of amusement. Now his eyes were cold, like blue chips of glass.

He came further into the room, closing the door forcefully behind him, moving with the unconscious male grace Clare remembered. 'Well?' he demanded abruptly.

Clare swallowed hard, too vulnerable after the memories that had just come flooding back to her, fighting for the coolness and assurance she was now known for. 'I'm going to be there,' she began.

'Oh yes?' His mouth twisted, his arms folded in challenge across his broad chest. 'And just when were you thinking of turning up?' he scorned.

She stood up, at once feeling more confident, knowing she was looking her best, deliberately so. Rourke might have hurt her in the past, but she was about to show him she was no longer the naïve girl she had been all those years ago. Having him come to her suite like this had caught her unawares.

'I was just on my way there,' she told him haughtily.

'Oh, were you?' he taunted. 'And I suppose the rest of us were supposed to be honoured by the fact that you were going to put in an appearance—even if it was late.'

'Late . . .?' She gave a hurried glance at her wrist-

watch. Two-thirty! She had been so caught up in her
memories she had forgotten the time. And Rourke was,
quite rightly, furious about it! 'I'm sorry——'

'Yeah, so am I,' he said impatiently. 'Jason told me
you were good to work with, that you had respect and
consideration for your fellow workers. I guess he was
talking with his body, not his mind.'

Clare gasped. 'What are you implying?'

Rourke shrugged. 'Jason's marriage is on the rocks,
maybe you helped it along a little.'

She saw red. No one had ever insulted her as much
as this man did! 'Just who the hell do you think you
are? I don't have to take these insults from you, you—
you——' she broke off. So much for remaining coolly
detached! 'I happen to be engaged.' This time she
managed to remain calm.

Harvey would be shocked if he had seen the way she
had just lost her temper. In the whole of the time she
had known him the nearest she had come to losing her
temper with him had been this morning, and she knew
the main reason for that had been this return to Los
Angeles.

Rourke eyed her mockingly. 'Does that ring on your
finger mean you don't sleep with anyone else?'

Her eyes flashed pure gold. 'It means I don't sleep
with—anyone else,' she amended her denial of sleeping
with anyone, full stop. Rourke would only mock the
fact that she and Harvey hadn't made love. Sex was just
an appetite to him, like eating or drinking. It didn't
mean a thing to him—and she should know!

'Lucky fiancé,' he drawled. 'Now, if it isn't asking
too much of the big movie star, could we get to work?'

She flushed. 'Of course. I'm sorry, I—I lost all track
of time.' Her tone was cool.

'So am I.' He opened the door for her. 'And if it happens again, little lady, I won't stop to ask why, I'll just
chew you out.'

What did he think he had done this time!

Clare's head was held high as they went down to the Windsor Room, Rourke scorning the use of the lift and taking the stairs. Clare followed him with a grace that wasn't in the least affected, her legs almost as long as his.

Rourke seemed deep in thought, and it gave her a chance to look at him undetected. She had been wrong about him, there were other changes besides his eyes, the lazy charm replaced with a grim determination, a purpose about him that she hadn't seen before.

'Do you like directing?' she heard herself ask.

'Yes,' he replied abruptly. 'Do you like acting?'

If she had been asked that question before accepting the role of Caroline she would probably have said yes without hesitation, but things were different now. Just being in the same city as Rourke and her mother was changing her way of thinking.

'I'll be glad to get back to London,' she answered evasively.

'Of course,' he nodded. 'You've been living there.'

Her mother had probably told him that—possibly when they were in bed together. God, how bitter she still was! But at eighteen, at any age, it was hard to accept that the man you loved was your mother's lover.

The Windsor Room was full of the cast and crew being used on the film. Rena gave her a wave from the back of the room, pointing to the empty seat next to her. Clare gratefully sat down on it, instantly feeling less conspicuous, although several people were looking at her rather curiously. Rourke took his place on the low platform at the other end of the room, and everyone suddenly fell silent.

'Miss Anderson was feeling rather tired after her flight,' he excused.

Clare looked at him with wide eyes, surprised he had made excuses for her. He had never been one to suffer fools gladly, and this new Rourke seemed even less tolerant.

But he was talking now, the usual pep-talk given by a director to the people who would work under him, explaining the necessity for punctuality at all times—a dig Clare felt made directly at her, although he didn't even glance in her direction. He went on to talk of the importance of the deadline for the film, the need for everyone to be aware of his or her lines for a particular scene. He was an arresting director, decisive and to the point, and she could see everyone in the room was listening to him intently, some with open respect in their eyes.

Respect was something she could never have for him, not as a man anyway. Any respect or love she might have had for him had died the night she found him in bed with her mother.

After the party, the way she had acted with Rourke, she had thought she must have overdone the cool act, for she had not seen him again for the next couple of weeks. Then her mother gave a party. She was going to London for a fortnight on location for the film she was presently working on, and so she threw a party for all her friends on the eve of her flight. Rourke was one of those friends.

Clare had been hoping he would be, and dressed accordingly. It was a new dress, bought specifically for the occasion, a clinging gold trifle that clung to all her provocative curves, bringing out the highlights in her hair, the honey tint to her skin from hours spent in the sun.

She looked, and felt, good, and she wanted Rourke to think the same thing. She was more attracted to him than to any other man she had met, and while she knew it was a dangerous interest she couldn't seem to help herself, had constantly looked out for him the last two weeks.

As the evening wore on and Rourke didn't put in an appearance her spirits began to flag. Gene had long since despaired of her uninterest in doing anything but sitting in the corner of the room, and had gone off with one of the other girls in the crowd they went about with. Clare didn't mind in the least, knowing she was poor company for anyone—other than Rourke.

Her mother was the life and soul of the party as usual, and Clare couldn't help but look at her with admiration. The flaming red dress she wore should have clashed with the brightness of her hair, and yet somehow it didn't, giving her a more exotic look than usual. Perry stood in the background, looking on in amusement as her mother charmed all the young men who flocked around her. Like a queen holding court, Clare thought once again.

She knew the instant Rourke came into the room, felt a tingling sensation all over her body. Once again he wasn't alone. The girl on his arm this time was a popular singer, her hair the same ebony as his, her face provocatively beautiful, from the full pouting mouth to the invitation in her eyes, eyes that didn't seem to leave her partner.

Clare had eyes only for Rourke too. Dressed all in black this evening, the shirt unbuttoned to his navel, he looked disturbingly attractive, his trousers once more skin-tight, showing each powerfully muscled line of his legs and thighs. Judy Lee obviously thought him too attractive to share, and clung to his arm as if she would never let go.

Clare turned away. Fool, fool, *fool*! Rourke hadn't been seriously interested in her, he just enjoyed teasing her whenever they did happen to meet. And she was breaking her heart for him, sure that she had fallen in love for the first time.

'Hello, Sunshine.'

She turned eagerly at the sound of his voice, unable to stop herself. 'Rourke!' She didn't even try to hide her pleasure.

'Hi,' he drawled in that lazy voice that she loved so much. 'Enjoying yourself?' He sat down next to her, his long legs stretched out in front of him, swirling the amber-coloured liquid around in his glass as he looked at her.

She hadn't been, but she was now, giving him a dazzling smile. 'Yes,' she said breathlessly, drinking in her fill of him after two weeks of not seeing him.

Rourke nodded. 'Where's your boy-friend?'

'Boy . . .? You mean Gene?' she frowned. 'But he isn't my boy-friend.'

His brows rose. 'That wasn't the impression you gave me the last time we spoke together.'

She flushed. 'No, well . . . You said you would go slowly with me,' she reminded him of the first time they had met. 'You've been anything but slow.'

For a moment he looked stunned, then he smiled, a slow, amused smile. 'Can you blame me?' He looked pointedly at the way her dress clung to her, her shoulders bare.

'Wouldn't you say suggesting we go to bed together at our first meeting was going a little fast?' she said dryly. 'Even for a sex symbol?'

'Honey, I've had girls ask to go to bed with me two minutes after we've been introduced,' he told her without conceit.

She could believe that. Rourke had a sensuality that women were drawn to. 'But we've never been properly introduced, have we?' she flirted.

He grinned. 'No, we haven't.' He laughed as she blushed. 'The way we met wasn't conducive to introductions, was it?'

'No,' Clare agreed huskily.

He moved impatiently, looking around the room with narrowed eyes. 'Are you really enjoying yourself?'

She made a face. 'No.'

Rourke gave her a thoughtful look. 'If I ask you to leave with me are you going to turn me down again?'

She smiled, her heart beating erratically. 'Have you ever been turned down three times?'

He ran one of his hands ruefully about the back of his neck, grimacing. 'Would it sound conceited if I said

I'd never been turned down twice?'

'No,' she gave a happy laugh. 'And at least I have that distinction.'

'And?'

'I'll get my jacket.'

Rourke shook his head. 'You won't need one. You can get a bikini—if you want one.'

Clare blushed as she remembered that he preferred to bathe in the nude. 'I'll get one,' she said breathlessly, hurrying from the room.

She had no idea what this evening alone was going to lead to, she only knew she wanted to be with Rourke for as long as he wanted her around, and for the moment he did seem to want that.

He was waiting in the hallway for her when she came downstairs, having changed out of the dress into a yellow tee-shirt and a tight-fitting yellow denims, the straightness of their style emphasising the slender length of her legs.

'Changed your mind about the costume?' He eyed her empty hands.

'I have it on underneath,' she blushed.

'Pity,' he drawled. 'Okay, let's go.'

Clare followed him out to the low black sports car, the roof down in the heat of the evening. Rourke opened the door for her with a flourish, kissing her briefly on the mouth before moving round to his own side of the car and swinging in behind the wheel. Within minutes they were driving along the coast road.

'What's so funny?' He eyed the smile on her lips questioningly.

'You are.'

'Me?'

'Mm,' she still smiled. 'I had a bet with myself that you wouldn't be able to sit down in the car in those trousers.'

Rourke gave a shout of laughter. 'Funny, I had the

same bet—about you.' His laughter deepened as she blushed.

'Does any women ever win with you?' she frowned. 'Even verbally?'

'You mean they couldn't physically?' he mocked.

'Yes—I mean no!' She gave a chagrined sigh. 'Do you tease all your women like you tease me?' she scowled.

'Are you my woman?' he asked softly.

'I—You—You know I am,' she admitted in a whisper.

His hand came out to clasp with hers, their fingers entwined as he lifted her hand to his lips, kissing each fingertip with erotic intensity. 'I didn't know, Clare,' for once he was completely serious. 'I just hoped.' He released her hand.

'Did you really?' All her decisions to remain distant and cool with him flew out of the window.

'Yes.'

'Oh, Rourke!' She gave him a glowing smile.

'Are you sure the nuns wouldn't be shocked again?' he teased to ease the tension.

'I know they would,' she said in a happy voice, loving the way the light breeze coming off the ocean ruffled his black curls into even more disorder, her own hair whipping lightly about her face. 'But I don't care,' she added with a touch of rebellion, sure that if Sister Teresa, a girl only a few years older than her, had met Rourke before she took her vows, she would never have taken them. He was as handsome as the devil, and as tempting. Goodness, was that being irreverent? She had a feeling it was. 'Will Miss Lee mind?' she changed the subject. 'After all, you did arrive with her.'

His mouth twisted derisively. 'And I thought you hadn't even noticed me!'

'Oh, I noticed,' she admitted throatily. 'Will she mind? Your going off with me, I mean.'

'Probably.'

Clare's eyes widened. 'Don't you care?'

'Not particularly,' he said in a bored voice.

Was she being a fool after all? Rourke treated his women as casually as he treated the rest of his life. She hadn't even seen him with the same woman twice. Was she being a fool to hope that with her it would be different, that Rourke would continue to see her after tonight?

'What about your mother?' he was asking now.

'Mummy . . .?'

'Yes—Mummy. Isn't she going to have something to say about you disappearing into the night with a man old enough to be your father?' he taunted.

'Oh, you aren't!'

'Believe me,' he nodded, 'I am.'

'Oh.' She frowned.

Rourke laughed softly. 'I made love for the first time at fourteen.'

'Oh,' she said once again, colour flooding her cheeks.

'Now I've shocked you!'

'Not at all,' she replied coolly. 'I—I just started a little later than you,' she invented.

'How old?'

'Er—Sixteen,' she made up. He would run a mile if he knew she was a *virgin*!

'Did you like it?'

Heavens, she wished she had never started this deception, finding it was becoming more and more embarrassing by the moment. 'Yes,' she answered stiffly.

'Don't worry,' once again his hand claimed hers, 'I'm not going to ask for details—just as I don't expect you to.'

'It would take you all night if I did,' she said tartly, pulling her hand away to stare sightlessly in front of her, hating all the other women he had made love to.

'Let's get one thing straight, Clare,' his voice was harsh. 'I'm not going to make any claims on you, and I don't expect you to make any on me. All right?' he rasped.

'All right,' she agreed moodily, staring out over the ocean. 'Does that mean that to you I'm just a one-night stand?'

'No!'

'Good,' she almost spat the word at him. 'Because I don't make love after only one date!'

Rourke looked at her with cold eyes. 'Did I say I wanted to make love to you?'

She swallowed hard. 'I—Well, you—No,' she admitted miserably. 'Not tonight,' she added defensively.

He gave an impatient sigh, running a hand through his unruly dark curls. 'Well, I do,' he said grimly.

Her eyes widened. 'You—you do?'

'Yes! But I don't expect it to be tonight. When it does happen it will just—happen. And it will be beautiful for both of us.'

She bit her lip, putting her hand on his thigh. 'I'm sorry, Rourke. I didn't mean to be bitchy.'

'Let's just forget it,' he dismissed tersely, moving her hand. 'And don't do that, not after the conversation we've just had.'

Clare knew he was trying to infuse lightness into the conversation, so she gave him a strained smile. 'Where are we going?'

'Nowhere.' He turned the car into a long driveway. 'We're there.' He switched off the ignition before getting out of the car.

Clare joined him after he had opened the door for her. They were at a beach house—at Malibu Beach! All the times she had been here with Gene the last few weeks, and Rourke had lived here all the time!

'Yes, I've seen you,' he answered her unasked question, opening the door to switch on all the lights, going inside he threw his car keys down on the coffee table. 'You make a handsome couple,' his mouth twisted. 'A golden couple.'

She looked about her appreciatively, loving the informality of her surroundings. Books and magazines lay on the furniture and wooden floor, scatter rugs on the latter; the furniture was all wicker, gay coloured cushions adding to its attractiveness. A corridor to the right of the room seemed to lead to the bedrooms, and two large glass doors opened out on to the patio area that overlooked the ocean. Rourke moved to open them, the breeze cool, the lights from the beach-house reflecting on the water.

She looked back at Rourke. 'Gene and I are only friends—I told you.'

'So you did,' he nodded. 'If you would like to strip off to your bikini I'll go and change.'

Clare walked out to the patio area once he had gone off to his bedroom, liking the simplicity with which Rourke had decorated his home. It wasn't exactly what she had been expecting, being used to the more luxurious homes of her mother's other friends. But she was glad Rourke lived less opulently; she hated the artificiality she had discovered this time she was home. It was a relief just to be somewhere she could relax.

By the time Rourke joined her, wearing navy blue swimming trunks, she had taken off her denims and tee-shirt to reveal the yellow bikini she wore underneath.

His eyes darkened as he looked at her. 'Do you do it on purpose?' he asked as he joined her on the patio, sitting down on the lounger next to hers.

'Do what on purpose?' She blinked her puzzlement.

'Wear yellow or gold. Are you trying to create an image?'

'No,' she laughed. 'Although it wouldn't be a bad idea. No, I always wear clothes that reflect my mood— bright colours mean I'm happy,' she told him truthfully.

'I'm glad,' he said huskily. 'Would you like a drink?'

'No, thanks.'

He looked at her intently. 'Do you take drugs?'

'Certainly not!' she gasped her shock. 'Do you?'

'Never,' he said grimly.

'Then why——'

'It wouldn't be so unusual,' he interrupted harshly. 'Everyone connected with this business seems to be addicted to something—drugs, booze, sex, or maybe just power,' he shrugged dismissively.

'I don't need to ask which one you're addicted to!'

'Don't you?' His eyes were cold.

'No!'

He gave a weary sigh. 'You don't even know me, Clare. And you shouldn't make snap judgments about people.' He stood up, holding out his hand to her. 'Let's go and swim.'

She put her hand into his, allowing him to pull her to her feet, frowning heavily. Rourke was turning out to be much more complex than she had realised; the lazy charm he presented to the world hid a man of many facets, not least his derision for a lot of his fellow-actors.

'Clare?' he interrupted her disturbing thoughts.

She looked up at him, forcing a smile to her suddenly stiff lips. 'Let's go and swim,' she agreed brightly.

He seemed about to say something else, then changed his mind, running agilely down the patio steps down on to the beach, pulling her with him.

She was laughing breathlessly by the time they reached the water's edge.

'Won't it be cold now that the sun's gone down?' She hung back.

'Yes,' he replied happily. 'It's nicer this way. And there are no noisy tourists to spoil the peace and quiet.'

Clare tentatively followed him into the water, gasping with shock. 'It's freezing!'

'Of course it isn't,' he chuckled, ducking completely under the water, his bronzed shoulders glistening as he stood up again. 'Don't be a baby,' he encouraged.

She gently lowered herself beneath the water, shuddering as she stood up again. 'Have you lived here long?' she shivered.

'Oh, I don't live here—at least, not all the time, and
not at all as far as the general public is concerned. I
have a house in Bel Air.'

'Up on the hill?'

'Up on the hill,' he nodded. 'Now, did you come out
here to swim or talk?'

Neither, if the truth be known. And some of what she
was feeling must have shown on her face, for Rourke
moved towards her with a muttered groan of her name.
He pulled her effortlessly into his arms and his mouth
came down to claim hers.

Clare curved herself shamelessly against him, the force
of the water propelling them even closer together, almost
knocking her off balance as she clung to him. But
Rourke stood as firm as a rock, supporting her weight
against him, all the time plundering her mouth with
ruthless insistence.

She could feel the rapid beat of his heart against her,
knew that he was as deeply affected as she was. His lips
moved slowly over her throat as she caressed his back
and shoulders, feeling the ripple of muscle beneath her
fingertips, then she groaned deeply in her throat as his
mouth once more possessed hers. Rourke's hands
moved pleasurably over her body, over her hips, her
waist and navel, one hand moving to cup her breast
over the silky material of her bikini top.

Her pulse raced, her breath came in short gasps as he
pushed the material aside to capture the firm contours
of her breast, his fingertips lingering on the hardened
nipple.

'I want to touch you, really touch you,' he gasped,
swinging her up in his arms to carry her out of the water,
laying her gently down on the sand before quickly joining her.

Her arms went about his neck as she pulled him down
to her, her legs entwined with his as his body pinned her
to the sand. She felt the catch released in the centre of
her breasts, the top discarded as Rourke's mouth moved

down to capture one hardened nipple between his teeth.

She had never known such ecstasy, had never dreamt there was such pleasure, holding Rourke against her as he slowly sucked and licked her breast. The rest of her body arched for those pleasure-giving lips, and she gasped as her other breast was captured in the warmth of his mouth, the nipple seeming to throb.

She was lost in such mindless pleasure that it seemed only natural, only right when his hand moved beneath her bikini briefs. But her eyes flew open in alarm as he touched her.

'What are you doing?' she gasped, stricken.

He frowned down at her with puzzled irritation. 'I'm loving you,' he said gruffly.

'I—But——' she licked her suddenly dry lips. 'No,' she shook her head, her eyes wide.

'No?'

'No!'

Rourke drew a deep controlling breath. 'No,' he agreed with a sigh, rolling off her to lie back on the sand, his arm thrown over his eyes. 'I'm sorry, Clare,' he murmured.

She swallowed hard, still breathing heavily herself, shocked by her behaviour. So much for her assertion that she didn't make love on the first date! It was only because of Rourke's control that they weren't making love now.

Suddenly he stood up, bending down to fasten her top before picking her up in his arms and walking into the water. When he had waded in deep enough he let her go.

Clare came up spluttering, indignation in every line of her body. 'What did you do that for?' she asked crossly, pushing the wet hair out of her eyes.

It was obvious from his own wet hair that he had ducked under the water himself. 'We both needed cooling off,' he said grimly. 'Come on, I think it's time I took you home.' He walked out on to the sand and back up to the house.

Clare slowly followed him, finding he had already disappeared into his bedroom by the time she got there, and towelled herself dry as best she could. She took the top off and pulled on her tee-shirt, not bothering to remove the briefs but pulling her denims on over the top of them. Her clothes clung to her damply.

But she needn't have worried; Rourke didn't even glance at her when he returned, his denims and tee-shirt as casual as her own, and picked up his car keys, ready to leave.

Clare felt tongue-tied on the drive back to her home, embarrassed at her inadequacy as a lover. Rourke had only been touching her, admittedly intimately, but considering she was supposed to be experienced she had behaved childishly.

'You aren't going to see me again, are you?' she said dully as he stopped the car in her mother's driveway.

Rourke turned to look at her, lifting a tendril of her damp hair. 'What makes you think that?' he murmured huskily.

'Well, I—Just now, I blew it, didn't I?'

He gave a mocking smile. '*I'm* the one who almost did that. You warned me not on the first date.'

Her expression brightened hopefully. 'Does that mean you will see me again?'

He gently touched her lips, tracing their peachy outline. 'The question is, will you see me?'

'Oh yes!' Her eyes were bright.

'Tomorrow?'

'Yes,' she nodded eagerly.

'I'll pick you up some time in the evening, but I'm not sure when. I'm filming at the moment, and we often run late. Okay?'

'Okay,' she glowed.

Rourke bent to kiss her lingeringly on the lips. 'Take care, Clare.'

She felt as if she floated into the house, where the

party was still in full swing, despite the lateness of the hour. She went straight up to her room, wanting to be alone to think about Rourke.

But she didn't get the chance, the door suddenly swinging open, slammed shut as her mother came into the room.

She looked Clare over speculatively, noticing everything about her, from her windswept hair to the way her clothes clung to her damply. 'Where have you been?' she demanded to know, her eyes flickering with fury.

Clare licked her lips nervously, never having seen her mother like this before. 'I—I went to the beach.'

'With Rourke?'

'I—Yes.'

'Are you mad?' her mother exploded, her face contorted with rage.

Clare flinched as if she had hit her. Her mother usually treated her with amused condescension, treating her almost as if she were eight instead of eighteen. And until this moment she had been happy to let her do so, happy in her mother's approval and affection. But it was different now, she was different. Rourke had made her feel like a woman, and she wanted to be treated like one, even by her mother.

She turned to the dressing-table and began to brush the tangles from her hair. 'I don't know what you mean——'

'Oh yes, you know,' her mother swung her round. 'Now listen to me, Clare, you are not to see Rourke Somerville again.'

She swallowed hard, frowning her surprise at her mother's vehemence. 'You have no right——'

'I have every right!' her mother firmly interrupted. 'The man is only interested in one thing——'

'Maybe I'm interested in the same thing,' Clare said defiantly, her head held high.

Her mother went pale with rage, her hand swinging up to slap Clare furiously across her cheek. 'Have you slept with him?' She shook Clare roughly by the shoulders.

'Not yet——'

'And you aren't going to!' her mother snapped. 'I want your promise here and now that you won't see him again.'

Clare's eyes glistened with unshed tears, as she cradled her throbbing cheek. 'I won't give such a promise,' she choked. 'It's unfair!'

'Then you'll come to England with me,' her mother told her firmly.

'I won't!' she cried. 'I want to stay here.'

'Not to see Rourke you won't,' she was told grimly. 'Now which is it to be, England with me, or your promise not to see Rourke again?'

'I don't understand you.' Clare's look was reproachful. 'I thought Rourke was a friend of yours?'

'He is. And that's exactly the reason I don't expect him to go around trying to seduce my daughter!' Carlene's mouth twisted angrily.

'I'm eighteen, Mummy——'

'And he's thirty-four!'

'But being eighteen gives me the right to decide whether or not that bothers me. And it doesn't.'

'That's only too obvious—*you're* only too obvious,' her mother added contemptuously. 'You're making a fool of yourself, Clare. And once Rourke has taken what he wants he'll leave you flat.'

Her head went back rebelliously. 'Maybe I'm willing to take that risk.'

'But I'm not. I'll have that promise, Clare, or you'll be on the plane with me tomorrow.'

Clare could tell by the determination in her mother's face that she meant what she said. Indignation warred with the lifelong habit of falling in with her mother's wishes. Those wishes had never seriously clashed with her own before, but she knew that for Rourke she would defy her mother a hundred times.

'You don't act this way about Gene,' she delayed.

'Gene is only a boy, and a gentleman, like his father,' the last was said somewhat contemptuously, making her wonder if her mother's relationship with Perry was as stable as she had thought it was.

She wondered what her mother would say if she knew the 'gentleman' she thought Gene to be had tried to make love to her on several occasions in the last few weeks. Not that there had ever been any doubt about her refusal, and Gene had accepted those refusals in good humour and continued to see her.

But she couldn't promise her mother she wouldn't see Rourke, not when just to think about him made her pulse race. 'What do you have against Rourke?' she wanted to know.

'I've just explained my reasons. He's too old for you, too experienced.'

'Maybe I like that.'

'Well, I don't!' her mother snapped.

'But, Mummy——'

'Clare,' Carlene interrupted firmly, 'I've given you the alternatives, my mind won't be changed about this.'

'All right.' Clare put her hands behind her back, crossing her fingers, not liking to lie, but knowing she had to if she wasn't to be taken away from Rourke. 'I won't see him again. There, are you satisfied?'

'Oh, Clare!' her mother hugged her. 'I'm only doing what I think is best for you.'

'Are you?' she said bitterly.

'Yes,' her mother smiled now that she had the promise. 'I worked with Rourke for a year, remember? I've seen him break too many girls' hearts to want to see my baby one of them.'

'You're sure you aren't jealous?' Clare paled even as she asked the question, wondering what had made her say such a thing.

'Jealous?' her mother echoed sharply. 'Why on earth should you say something like that?'

'I—I'm sorry,' she frowned. 'I don't know why I said it.'

Several emotions flickered across her mother's face, all of them too fleeting for Clare to recognise. Finally she smiled. 'All forgiven, darling. I realise you're upset. Rourke is such a devil. I'm sure he's made you infatuated with him already.' The last was almost a question.

Clare forced a casual shrug, sure that her mother would drag her off to England anyway if she knew how deeply involved with Rourke she already was, how much she loved him. And she did love him, she felt only truly alive in his company.

'He's exciting to be with,' she remarked casually.

Her mother smiled. 'You aren't the first young girl to be flattered to be seen with a famous movie star. But Rourke is not for you, I doubt he's for anyone.'

And so her mother had gone off to England, quite happily believing Clare wouldn't be seeing Rourke in her absence. Clare had hated the deception, but her love for Rourke was such that she had to be with him.

And she had been with him, constantly for the next two weeks, until her mother had returned and she learnt the true reason why she hadn't wanted her to see Rourke.

But her mother had been right about one thing; Rourke hadn't been for anyone. After five years he was still unmarried. She knew very little about his life these past years, except that he had branched out into directing, although he still acted too. Why not, she thought bitterly, he had a natural ability for it.

And there would have been women, hundreds of them. In five years, at the rate Rourke got through women, it would have to be hundreds!

'Does that meet your approval, Miss Anderson?'

She was once again jolted out of her memories by the sound of Rourke's voice. This time he was chillingly polite.

She looked selfconsciously about the room, finding

herself the cynosure of all eyes. She had no idea what Rourke had been talking about the last half an hour, just as she had no idea what was supposed to meet her approval.

A delicate pink coloured her cheeks, and she licked her lips nervously. 'I beg your pardon?' she returned with equal coolness.

By the tightening of his mouth she knew Rourke was aware of her inattentiveness. 'I have just informed everyone,' he emphasised the last, his eyes glacial, 'that only the most necessary staff will be present during the nude scenes. I was asking if that met your approval.'

Clare swallowed hard. The nude scenes—how could he talk about them so calmly!

Ever since she had learnt that he had taken Jason Faulkner's place she had pushed the thought of those love scenes to the back of her mind. But now they came back with alarming clarity, Caroline and Gunther in bed together, making love.

And just what did Rourke mean, did that meet her approval! Did he imagine she wanted everyone to see them in bed together?

CHAPTER FOUR

'MISS ANDERSON?' he questioned tautly.

'Yes,' her voice was stilted, 'of course that meets my approval.'

'Good,' he snapped. 'Now perhaps we can all call it a day.' He gathered up the papers in front of him as the rest of them stood up and filed out of the room.

'Phew!' Rena breathed at Clare's side. 'He was a bit rough on you.'

Rourke hadn't been rough at all. She hadn't been listening, he had a right to be annoyed. And he had been, his eyes like ice, his expression harsh.

'I deserved it,' she shrugged, aware that Rourke was still somewhere in the room behind them. Nevertheless, she jumped nervously when he suddenly appeared at her side.

'I'm glad you realise it,' he said grimly, showing her that he had been walking behind her for some time. 'I'd like to talk to you,' he added abruptly.

'See you later,' Rena said goodnaturedly, and left them alone.

Clare eyed Rourke warily. 'What do you want to talk about?'

'Not here,' he rasped, taking hold of her elbow and propelling her towards the stairs, once again shunning the use of the lift.

She swallowed hard, not wanting him to see how much he still alarmed her. 'I don't see what we can possibly have to talk about,' she told him coolly. 'Besides, I'm meeting my fiancé.'

Rourke's mouth twisted contemptuously. 'What I have to say is strictly business, honey,' he drawled. 'Nothing your fiancé couldn't sit in on if he wanted to.'

Her mouth set mutinously. She didn't want to be alone with this man—and she had no idea why it bothered her so much. She was going to marry Harvey, and yet Rourke's hold on her arm disturbed her, just being with him disturbed her!

He went back to her suite, waiting with ill-concealed impatience while she unlocked the door. Once inside Clare threw the key on to the coffee-table and turned to face Rourke with a confidence she was far from feeling.

'What do you want to talk about?' she asked once again.

Rourke sat down without being asked to do so, running a tired hand over his furrowed brow. 'Do you have any idea how difficult it is for me to take over the direction of this film at such short notice?' he asked.

Whatever she had been expecting him to say it hadn't been that, and her eyes widened in astonishment. 'I—Well, I—I never thought about it.'

'No, I don't suppose you did. Well it is, damn difficult. And it isn't helped by your prima donna act,' he added harshly.

Clare paled. 'By my . . .?'

'Yes!' He stood up, pacing the room. 'I'm aware that you don't like me, that you would rather have someone else working on this movie with you—but you've got *me*. And showing your contempt for me by not even paying attention to what I'm saying isn't going to get you anywhere with me.'

She gasped. 'But I—That isn't what happened,' she protested.

His nostrils flared out angrily. 'Isn't it?'

'No! I——' She put a hand up to her temple, pushing her hair back as it tumbled about her face. 'I was tired——'

'I already made that excuse for you,' his mouth twisted.

'It was the true one!'

'Then maybe you should try sleeping alone once in a while,' he rasped.

Clare had never been so incensed, her image of coolness flew out of the window. 'Mind your own damned business!' Her eyes sparkled rebelliously.

'It is my business if your tiredness affects the making of this movie.'

'I only flew in today——'

'And whose fault is that? You've known for weeks that you had to be here by today. And I know for a fact that you've been in London since you finished your last film a month ago.'

She didn't ask how he knew, sure that he wouldn't tell her even if he did. And the reason she had left it so late arriving in Los Angeles was because she had wanted to delay for as long as possible the painful memories she was going through today.

'I'm here,' she said stiffly, 'and that's all that matters.'

'No, it isn't all that matters, damn you!' He turned on her angrily. 'You and Jason went through a lot of the scenes you have together when you were in England?'

'Of course.' She gave a haughty inclination of her head, thinking of all the hours they had wasted.

Rourke's eyes glittered angrily. 'And didn't it occur to you that we could have spent the last week or so doing the same thing?'

'Of course it didn't! I had no idea——' She broke off, biting her lip, unwilling to let him know just how vulnerable she was.

His eyes narrowed to steely slits, his expression wary. 'No idea of what?'

'It didn't occur to me,' she shrugged dismissively.

'No idea of what?' he repeated determinedly.

Clare swung away from him, sure that she would never again regain her composure. 'I didn't know you were to be the director,' she admitted with a sigh.

'Didn't know . . .? *Why* didn't you know?'

'I had no idea Jason—I wasn't told,' she explained lamely.

'So you didn't know until you arrived here today that I was to be here too?' Rourke said slowly.

'No.'

For the first time today she saw humour lighten his expression, saw some of the devil lurking in his deep blue eyes. 'Were you shocked, little baby?' he taunted softly.

'I was a little—surprised.'

'I'm sure you were,' he chuckled wryly.

'Don't worry,' she flashed. 'I have no intention of taking advantage of our past—association.'

The humour faded, his mouth curled back into a sneer. 'Honey, we didn't have an *association*. We had sex, once,' he rasped. 'And it wasn't even that good.'

Clare felt as if he had hit her, her face going a sickly grey colour. 'It wasn't once,' she choked. 'It was twice.' And he was right, it hadn't been good, not the first time anyway. She had been too inexperienced, had panicked at the last moment, and Rourke had been too aroused to stop. He had hurt her, badly. But the second time had been so good she had cried with happiness. Obviously, it hadn't affected Rourke in the same way.

'Was it?' he said in a bored voice. 'I don't remember.'

She held back her tears with an effort, knowing that once he had left the room the floodgates would open up. It was a long time since she had cried, and it had been because of Rourke that time too.

'I thought you said my fiancé could sit in on this conversation,' she reminded him stiffly, knowing that Harvey would be shocked out of his mind if he could hear what they had been talking about.

'So?'

'So you've been very—personal,' she blushed, the greyness started to recede.

Rourke shrugged. 'He must know there was someone else before him.'

Clare blinked. 'He must?'

'Don't tell me you thought he didn't know,' Rourke scorned. 'Every man can tell when he's the first.'

'And you should know!' she said bitterly.

'And I should know,' he nodded distantly. 'Do you think you're going to be able to handle this, Clare?'

She wouldn't be able to handle anything in a moment, she would burst into tears in front of him—and she was determined not to do that. 'Working with you, you mean?' she asked quietly.

'Yes.'

Her head was held at a proud angle. 'I can handle it. After all, you were only the first, Rourke,' her mouth twisted. 'You're far from being the last.'

'I know that,' he rasped harshly. 'Just make sure you get *some* sleep tonight. We start at seven sharp in the morning,' he reminded her.

'I'll be there.'

'I'll make damned sure you are,' he said grimly. 'I've never approved of families getting involved on location,' he muttered.

'That's because you don't have any.' Her remark was made to wound, and she knew she had succeeded by the whiteness about Rourke's mouth. She instantly felt contrite. 'I'm sorry, Rourke——'

'So am I,' he snapped. 'Sorry I ever told you anything about my life. Goodbye!' and he slammed out of the room.

Clare sank down into the nearest chair—something she seemed to have been doing all day today, as one trauma piled on top of another.

She vividly remembered the night Rourke had told her about his childhood, remembered it because it was also the night he had become her lover!

Her mother was to be in England for two weeks, and she managed to see Rourke every single day of that two weeks, even if it was only for a short time. He hadn't lied when he said he was busy filming, and often he didn't finish until nine or ten o'clock at night, only giving them time to have a snack supper together before Rourke collapsed into bed, building up his energy for the next day's filming.

Not once did he ask her to share that bed, be it at the beach-house or his more luxurious home in Bel Air. He kissed her, and touched her, but never with the same intensity he had that night on the beach.

And it was driving her insane! She knew that she couldn't stand his casual attitude to their relationship much longer, and on the eve of her mother's expected return she knew she didn't have a moment to lose. Because Rourke preferred his privacy and as he was also working hard, not many people had seen them together, but Clare knew that it wouldn't be long after her mother's return that she would find out about her and Rourke. And she wasn't sure enough of Rourke's feelings for her to know whether he would withstand the pressure her mother would put to bear.

That last evening she dressed with special care, wanting Rourke to desire her, knowing that once her mother returned things would never be the same between them again.

Rourke's eyebrows rose when he called for her at eight o'clock, and she knew he approved of the yellow dress, of its fitted bodice, the way her pointed breasts supported the material, her shoulders completely bare, the style straight and fitted over her waist and hips, a long slit up the left side of the dress giving her freedom of movement—otherwise she doubted she would have been able to walk, the dress fitted her so snugly.

'What's the occasion?' drawled Rourke, opening the car door for her.

'No occasion,' she denied, flushing with pleasure at the way his eyes darkened over the long expanse of thigh that had been revealed as she sat down. 'I just wanted to look nice for you,' she added as he got in beside her.

'And you do.' He made no effort to start the engine,

turning towards her. 'But I thought we were having a barbecue at the beach-house tonight?' He was dressed very casually in denims and a sweat-shirt.

'We are,' she frowned her puzzlement.

'Then why—Never mind,' he shook his head dismissively, flicking the key in the ignition, the engine roaring into life.

Clare pouted her disappointment. 'If you would rather I changed——'

'Certainly not,' he turned to smile at her as they drove out to the beach road. 'You look beautiful enough to eat.'

That was the whole idea! The past two weeks she had rarely worn a dress, the casualness of their dates calling for either shorts, or alternatively denims and a top. Tonight she had wanted to show him she could look beautiful if she wanted to, and she was disappointed by his reaction.

The hand nearest to her moved out as he gently touched her cheek. 'You look lovely, Clare,' he told her throatily.

Pleasure instantly lit up her eyes. 'I do?'

'Yes,' he smiled, his hand returning to the steering-wheel. 'But with you looking like that I think I should change and take you out to eat.'

'No! I mean, no, I—I'd much rather have the barbecue.' If they ate out he would simply drive her home afterwards, and that wasn't what she wanted at all. Besides, she liked him in the black denims and sweat-shirt, sure that he had never looked more ruggedly handsome than he did at this moment.

'Sure?' he frowned.

'Very sure,' she nodded eagerly.

'Okay,' he shrugged, 'barbecue it is.'

By the time the steaks were cooked and the salad tossed and put on the table on the sun-deck the sun had gone down and the sky was a bluish black as they sat down to eat their meal, the only sound the soft music coming from the stereo in the lounge, and the crash of the waves against the sand.

Clare smiled dreamily as she ate her meal, sure that she would never be happier than she was right now. Everything was perfect—the meal, the wine, Rourke sitting opposite her, his mood relaxed and teasing. He wasn't always this relaxed, it often took him a couple of hours to lose his tension after a day's filming, and she remarked on how hard he worked.

Rourke shrugged. 'I was taught at the orphanage that if someone pays you to do a job then it's up to you to do it, no matter how long it takes to get it right.'

'Tell me about it,' she prompted softly; the subject of his childhood had never been entered into before.

Normally he would teasingly have changed the subject, but tonight his mood was mellowed by the wine. He began to talk. 'My mother was a rich American woman, my father a poor Irish gardener—her gardener. I think my mother must have liked the look of the rough Irish labourer, because they became lovers.'

'And you're the result of their marriage?'

His mouth twisted. 'They didn't get married, Clare. My mother couldn't marry an Irish immigrant, it was beneath her. No, he was only good enough to share her bed, not to become her husband.'

'You can't know that——'

'Oh, can't I?' he rasped bitterly. 'I can assure you I know exactly how my mother felt about my father and me. She came to see me once, at the orphanage,' his eyes were distant, looking into the past. 'She had married some wealthy American businessman, a man of wealth *and* breeding. She had two other children, both of them a lot younger than me, but she wanted to do something for the bastard she had brought into the world. She put some money into trust for me that I could claim on my twenty-first birthday.'

Clare was shocked and dismayed by what he was telling her. He would have been better never to have met his mother, at least that way he could have made excuses for her rejection. 'And did you—did you claim the money?'

'No,' he gave a bleak smile. 'Much as I thought the bitch owed me something I didn't want her damned money.'

'And—and have you ever seen her again?'

'Never,' he said in an uncompromising voice.

'And your father?'

'Dead,' he rasped.

'I—How?'

Rourke's mouth twisted with bitter humour. 'I'd like to be able to tell you that he wasted away for love of my mother, but it wouldn't be true. He married some other woman, and he died an alcoholic when I was five years old. My mother told me all about it.'

'Oh, Rourke, I'm so sorry!' She reached out and clasped the hand that kept clenching and unclenching as he told of his childhood so different from her own cushioned one. 'But I suppose there is one thing, your mother didn't have to have you. I mean, there must have been abortion, even then.'

'Not for a Catholic,' he rasped. 'So she had me and stuck me in an orphanage.'

'Oh, Rourke,' she choked. 'Rourke, I——'

'Let's have some more wine,' he suggested in a reckless voice, standing up. 'We've talked enough for one day.'

'Yes.' Clare followed him into the house, wishing she had never asked him to talk of his past. He was still very bitter, blamed his mother for his rejection. No wonder he treated women so casually, with such a woman for a mother!

They sat in the lounge listening to the stereo, Rourke staring broodingly into space, neither of them attempting to make conversation.

Finally Clare couldn't stand it any more, and stood up to leave. 'I think I'd better go.' She smoothed her dress down over her hips, slipping her feet back into her sandals.

'No!' Rourke stood up too. 'No ... I'm sorry I'm such bad company, Clare. How about if we go for a swim, clear the cobwebs?'

Her expression brightened. 'Okay,' she nodded.

He bent and kissed her lightly on the lips. 'I'll go and change, you'll find some spare costumes in that cupboard. I keep them for unexpected—visitors.'

She looked in the cupboard once he had gone into his bedroom, finding half a dozen bikinis in assorted colours and sizes. He was prepared for everything—or every woman!

Well, she would see if he was prepared for this! She ignored all the bikinis, rapidly shedding her clothes before running across the golden sand into the dark blue water.

Rourke came down the sand a few minutes later, swimming out to join her. 'You should have waited for me,' he told her sternly. 'I wondered where the hell you were until I saw this golden mane.' He wound a strand of her hair about his fingers, pulling her closer.

'Did you?' she asked throatily, her arms going about his neck as she pressed herself against him.

'What the——! Clare?' he frowned down at her.

'Yes, darling?' She rained light kisses along his jaw.

'You don't have any clothes on!'

'No.' She gave a husky laugh, her hands moving down to his hips.

Rourke stiffened. 'What are you doing now?' His hands held hers immobile.

She kissed him lingeringly, her tongue running lightly along the edge of his parted lips. 'If we take off your bathing trunks,' she murmured softly, 'you'll be naked too.'

His mouth twisted derisively as he refused to release her hands. 'And then what happens?'

'You make love to me—I hope.' She met his searching gaze unflinchingly.

'I do?' His eyebrows rose.

'I hope so,' she nodded.

'Clare——'

She entwined her legs with his, feeling his arousal against her thigh. 'We're a long way past the first date,' she reminded him huskily.

Rourke's eyes darkened. 'So we are,' he agreed softly. 'Okay, go ahead,' he released her hands.

She was glad of the darkness to hide her blushes, suddenly feeling very shy as she moved the bathing trunks down his body, aware of every muscle and sinew as she held the black trunks triumphantly in the air.

'Throw them away,' Rourke instructed throatily, moving closer to her in the water.

'Throw them . . .?'

'Mm,' he murmured against her throat, as their bodies fused together.

Clare gave a nervous laugh, watching as the piece of black material bobbed off into the distance. 'Someone's imagination is going to be working overtime when they find them,' she said jerkily, as the full force of what she had invited suddenly washed over her.

Rourke's eyes were dark as he looked down at her. 'As long as they come to the right conclusion.'

She swallowed hard, feeling the fierce beat of his heart beneath her hand, the power of his thighs telling her how badly he wanted her. 'Which is?'

He ran the tip of his tongue along the edge of her mouth. 'That tonight I'm a very lucky man.'

Her eyes glowed as she opened her mouth to his, holding nothing back as she returned his kiss. Rourke kissed her slowly, druggingly, igniting a fire within her that set her body on fire, her arms clinging to him where she couldn't touch the sandy ocean floor.

But kisses weren't enough for either of them, and soon Rourke was taking her hand to lead her out of the water and back to the beach-house.

Clare drank in the sight of him, from his broad

shoulders down his tapered waist, to the full arousal of his thighs. He looked like some bronzed pagan god, and she trembled with the anticipation of being possessed by such a man.

They walked through the darkened beach-house to Rourke's bedroom, Clare looking up adoringly as he gently laid her on the bed, looking at her as she had looked at him seconds earlier, slowly taking in every naked inch of her body, as if memorising it for future reference.

'You're one beautiful lady,' he told her huskily.

She gave a shaky laugh and pulled him down to her. 'And you're one beautiful man,' she murmured, instigating the deep kiss, but not minding in the least when Rourke took control, his fierce passion taking her breath away.

But he didn't want to just kiss her mouth, not even taking her when she begged him to, his lips and hands exploring every inch of her body before he moaned low in his throat.

'Now, Clare,' he groaned. 'It has to be *now*.'

As his body moved over hers something inside her seemed to shut off, an age-long fear of the pain a lot of her school friends had associated with 'the first time' coming to the fore. As Rourke's legs parted hers she began to struggle.

'No games, Clare,' he warned, past the stage of being able to pull back, his body totally committed to making love to her.

'I'm not playing——'

His expression was savage. 'Then you picked the wrong man to tease!' His body possessed hers with a fierceness that made her cry out her pain. 'My God! Clare . . .?' he choked, raising his head dazedly. 'Clare, are you—were you——'

'Yes!' she groaned, rigid with fear and pain.

He buried his face in her throat. 'God, Clare, I'm sorry,' he moaned. 'But it's too late now, too late . . .'

When it was all over Clare turned on her side, her back towards Rourke. He lay on his back, his breathing still ragged, staring sightlessly up at the ceiling.

'You should have told me,' he finally spoke.

'Yes,' she shuddered.

'You shouldn't have deceived me in that way.' His voice was harsh.

'No.'

'Clare——' He turned, putting his hand on her arm.

'Don't touch me!' She flinched away from him.

'All right, I won't,' he sighed, and the bed dipped slightly as he moved away from her. 'Sleep now. We'll talk in the morning.'

Surprisingly she did sleep, the tears drying on her cheeks as she slept. She woke to feel a warm, soft wall beneath her cheek, a tattoo tapping in her head. She blinked to clear her head, realising that the soft wall was Rourke's chest, the tattoo his heartbeat. She flinched away from him as she saw his eyes glittering down at her in the half-light of early morning.

'No, Clare,' he said firmly, refusing to let her move away. 'I've been waiting all night for you to wake up. Last time it was——'

'Last time?' she stared at him in panic.

'Yes.' He rolled over, pinning her to the bed beneath him. 'I didn't know—You should have told me you were a virgin. I would have been gentle with you—as I'm going to be this time.'

'No!' She began fighting him again, pushing him, scratching him, kicking him, anything to stop that painful invasion of her body for a second time.

'Clare!' He pinned both her arms above her head with one of his. 'Clare, you have to let me. I can't let it end like this——'

'It's already over,' she spat the words at him. 'It was over the minute you raped me.'

Rourke shook his head, very pale in dawn's morning light. 'It wasn't rape, Clare——'

'Wasn't it?' her eyes flashed pure gold. 'I remember it differently.'

He closed his eyes. 'I'm trying not to remember it at all,' he groaned, his eyes opening. 'Trust me, Clare. This time trust me.'

She stopped fighting and looked up at him pleadingly. 'I want to. But——'

'It will be all right.' He cupped either side of her face, gently kissing her eyes, her mouth. 'I'll make it all right.'

And he did. He was very patient with her, this time giving her no chance to be frightened, and when the pleasure came it was all the deeper for being unexpected. Her whole body felt as if it were bathed in a pleasurable glow, tears gently falling.

As she looked at him with tear-wet cheeks she knew that she still loved this man, last night forgotten in this morning's blaze of pleasure. It had been beautiful, wonderful—she couldn't begin to describe the ecstacy Rourke had given her with his gentleness.

But he was moving away from her and pulling on his clothes, his expression harsh.

Clare struggled to sit up. 'Rourke . . .?' she frowned as he buttoned his shirt, thrusting it into his denims.

He didn't even look at her. 'It's after six,' he said abruptly. 'I have to get to work.'

'But, Rourke——'

'Let yourself out when you're ready,' he continued coldly, pulling on a leather jacket. 'The door is self-locking, and I have the key.'

She swallowed hard. 'Rourke, are you leaving?'

'I just told you,' he shot her an impatient look, 'I have to get to work.'

Clare licked her suddenly dry lips. 'Will I see you again?'

'I don't think there would be any point in that,' he said harshly.

'You mean——'

'I mean it's over,' he rasped. 'It should never have

begun. There's some money on the dressing-table, take a taxi home.'

'Rourke . . .!' He didn't even hear her plea for him to stop, and the front door closed with a slam seconds later.

She looked at the money he had left, a hundred dollars in five twenties, just as if—as if—Oh God, she wanted to die!

She sobbed into the pillow. Her mother had been right, Rourke had taken what he wanted, had even left her money for it, and now he wasn't interested. Oh, she had been a fool, such a fool!

She got up and dressed, leaving immediately, the money still where he had left it. She never wanted to see Rourke or the beach-house again as long as she lived; she used her own money to get home.

By the time her mother returned late in the afternoon Clare was pale but composed, never wanting her mother to know how right she had been to warn her against Rourke.

It was as if their argument before her mother left had never happened, her mother seeming confident that she had kept her promise not to see Rourke. If only she had! She had known a few moments' pleasure in Rourke's arms, and now it seemed she would spend a lifetime of unhappiness without him.

Gene telephoned later that afternoon, and despite her wish to bury herself in a hole and die Clare knew she couldn't do that. Rourke had kicked her out of his life as if she were some cheap little whore he had picked up for the night. He hadn't been able to take the knock to his ego when she had only felt pain at his lovemaking, so he had put her through the further humiliation of making her enjoy it, of giving her ecstasy. She would never forget that final humiliation.

And so she accepted Gene's invitation to go out to dinner with him, feeling somewhat guilty about her neglect of him the last two weeks. He had called her several times, and each time she had refused, having a previously arranged date with Rourke.

'Rourke out of the picture now?' he quirked a questioning eyebrow at her as they ate dinner.

Clare was only picking at her food, mainly pushing it around her plate in a show of eating. She looked up sharply. 'Rourke?' she echoed.

He smiled. 'Don't try that big innocent-eyed act with me. It might work with your mother, but I know you've been seeing Rourke while she's been away.'

'I—How?'

Gene shrugged. 'I have ways.'

She gave a wan smile. 'You sound like part of the C.I.A.!'

Gene gave a soft chuckle. 'Believe me, that's almost what the gossip around here is like.'

They were seated in an ocean-side restaurant, but Clare had no appetite for the seafood, just the sound of the ocean brought back painful and humiliating memories of last night. If only Rourke hadn't completely subjugated her, made love to her the second time, she would at least have her pride to console her now.

But she had nothing, only the knowledge that she still loved Rourke—and after paying for a night with her he didn't even think her worth seeing again.

'I think I'd like to leave now, Gene,' she told him jerkily. 'I—I have a headache,' she invented.

'Okay,' he shrugged acceptance. 'Would you like to go for a drive?' he asked once they were outside. 'It would help clear your head.'

She would like to go home, but it was only ten-thirty, and if she returned home this early her mother would want to know the reason why. 'Lovely,' she smiled agreement.

She didn't talk at all on the long drive, didn't even know where they went, all she knew was that it was twelve o'clock by the time Gene finally stopped his car outside her home.

'Give it time, Clare,' he advised softly as she got out of the car.

She bit her bottom lip painfully. 'I don't know what you mean.'

'You know,' he contradicted gently. 'And you aren't the first woman to have loved unwisely.'

Her eyes flashed. 'I don't love Rourke!' she snapped.

'Don't you?'

'No!' She turned towards the house.

'I'll call you, Clare,' Gene called after her.

'Okay,' she accepted shakily, just wanting to get to the privacy of her room and sob her heart out.

But first she had to say goodnight to her mother. It was a nightly ritual when she had been out for the evening, discussing it with her mother when she got home. Tonight she intended cutting that chat short.

She tapped lightly on the bedroom door, feeling the handle turn before she could open it herself.

'Clare!' Her mother looked flustered, pulling her négligé about her, the black lacy garment suiting her colouring. 'I—er—I wasn't expecting you home yet.'

She frowned at her mother's agitation. 'I just came to say goodnight——' she broke off as she saw the dark head lying on one of the pillows in her mother's huge double bed, the black curls achingly familiar to her. 'Rourke...' she choked. 'My God, Rourke and—and *you*?' she looked accusingly at her mother.

Her mother came completely out of the bedroom, closing the door softly behind her. 'Don't make so much noise, dear, you'll wake him. He's had such a hard day at the studio.'

Clare felt sick, unable to believe what was happening. 'You and Rourke?' she repeated dazedly.

'Well, of course Rourke and I,' her mother confirmed impatiently. 'I thought you knew that.'

'No...' Was she going mad or was this really happening? It was like some horrendous nightmare! Rourke and her *mother*!

'Why do you think I warned you to stay away from him?' her mother derided.

'I thought you were worried about *me*,' Clare choked.

'I was, darling,' Carlene smiled, her auburn hair ruffled prettily about her face. 'Rourke is such a rogue, he can't resist trying to seduce every woman he meets.'

Anger burned deep within her, both at her mother and Rourke. 'Are you aware of the fact that he seduced me?' she asked tightly.

'He made a full confession,' her mother gave an affectionate laugh. 'Well, don't look so upset, Clare. I did warn you, and every girl has to start somewhere. At least you were taught by an expert.'

'And you should know,' she muttered.

'He's a very good lover, isn't he, Clare?'

'Is that all you have to say?' she choked.

'What else is there?' her mother shrugged. 'I think you should get to bed now, darling, it's very late. And don't disturb us in the morning, Rourke doesn't have to go to work tomorrow, so he can lie in if he wants to.' Her expression seemed to say he would want to, and not with the intention of sleeping either!

Clare didn't say another word, but turned on her heel and walked to her room. She had packed her suitcases and left within half an hour—and she hadn't seen either her mother or Rourke again until today.

Five years, five long years, and she could still remember every detail, every look, every touch. Not even Harvey, the man she was going to marry, had blotted out the memory of Rourke.

Oh God, Harvey! She had forgotten all about him during the last few hours, the past enwrapping her like a dark ominous cloud.

But it was over now. She had relived it, and by reliving it she had rekindled her active dislike and disgust of

Rourke. When she had got to England she had hated him with a passion, but as she got on with living her life that hate had faded to the background. Now it was back with a vengeance. She hated him and he couldn't touch her now, she wouldn't let him.

CHAPTER FIVE

SHE was calm now, and calmly she put in a call to Harvey, reminding him of their dinner date in her room.

'What time shall I be there?'

His unmistakable eagerness was the boost she needed to her dented confidence. 'Whenever you like,' she invited warmly.

'Now?' he asked huskily.

Clare laughed softly. 'If you want.'

'Did you rest yet?' he asked concernedly.

'Er—For a while,' she invented, remembering the excuse she had given Rourke for her lateness this afternoon. Not that she thought Harvey and Rourke were likely to compare notes, the two men total opposites, but she could no more tell Harvey the real reason for her lateness than she could Rourke. 'I'll tell you about it later,' she said briskly. 'Can you give me half an hour to shower and change?'

'But of course, darling,' he instantly agreed. 'But don't go to any trouble on my account, you know you always look beautiful to me.'

'Thank you, darling,' she said with sincerity. 'That's a really sweet thing to say.'

'It happens to be true,' he assured her softly.

She knew it, knew that to Harvey she was perfect. He had no idea of the blemish in her past, believing her to be an innocent. Rourke had said Harvey would know he wasn't the first with her, something that hadn't even occurred to her, so perhaps she owed it to Harvey to tell him the truth before they were married. Oh, not the name of the man involved, she could never tell anyone that, but the fact that there had been one other man in

87

her life. Yes, perhaps she owed him that.

'I'll see you later, Harvey,' she said warmly.

'I'll look forward to it.'

She dressed with care, freshly showered, her hair newly washed, straight and golden to just below her shoulders. She wore plum-coloured velvet trousers and a cream lace Victorian-style blouse tucked neatly in at the waist. She looked cool and confident, the way Harvey liked her to look.

Her kiss was possessive when he arrived exactly half an hour later, casually dressed himself in black fitted trousers and a white shirt, the collar of the latter turned back over his black velvet jacket. He looked very handsome, and Clare's heart warmed to him, as she returned his kiss with a warmth that made his draw back in surprise.

'Clare?' he frowned his puzzlement.

She smiled at him, almost on a level with his six feet in her high-heeled sandals. 'I missed you,' she said throatily.

'You did?'

'Yes,' she laughed softly at his surprise.

Harvey's arms tightened about her waist. 'That's nice.'

'I thought so,' she nodded.

His eyes darkened to a deep blue as he lowered his head to once more claim her lips, kissing her long and deeply.

She enjoyed Harvey's kisses, felt protected in his company, and yet she would be a fool if she didn't know that rockets didn't go off in her head when he kissed her, that she didn't melt in his arms when he touched her. But she also knew there was more to marriage than having a nerve-shattering lover for a husband. She respected Harvey, more than she could ever respect Rourke. She was confident she would make Harvey a good wife.

He seemed pleased by her reaction, his arm about her

shoulders as they sat together on the sofa. 'Hungry?' he asked teasingly.

She wasn't, but she was going to need all her strength to get through making this film. Checking the schedule she had found that she was on the set almost every day, and that meant every day in Rourke's company.

'Starving!' she exaggerated.

She curled up next to him as he ordered their dinner to be sent to the suite, feeling relaxed for the first time today.

'So, what do you think of Somerville?' Harvey asked the one question guaranteed to bring back her tension.

And it did. She sat up, her manner instantly constrained. 'He seems very—competent,' she replied stiffly.

'Oh, he is,' Harvey nodded. 'He won an award for best director last year.'

Clare knew that, she had seen the reports in the press. She also knew that he had appeared in several films the last few years, but she still hadn't been to see any of them. 'Then he must be good,' she said grudgingly.

'Very good,' Harvey nodded.

'I—I'm afraid I got off on the wrong foot with him.' She felt she owed Harvey some explanation for the coolness he was sure to detect between Rourke and herself.

He frowned. 'You did? But I've never known you not to get on with anyone.'

She explained about being late for the meeting, and how Rourke had come looking for her.

'I'm sure he understood,' Harvey said soothingly.

Clare knew Rourke hadn't 'understood' at all. 'You're probably right——'

'I'm sure I am. After all——' He didn't get any further, a loud knock on the door interrupted him. He stood up. 'That must be our dinner.'

It was, and the subject of Rourke Somerville was forgotten as they ate their meal. As they talked of less painful topics Clare was able to relax once again, eating a little, if not doing full justice to the lovely meal Harvey had ordered.

Harvey put the tray outside the door once they had finished. 'So that we aren't disturbed,' he said meaningly.

Clare was aware of the fact that she had been flirting more with Harvey this evening than she usually did, and that he had taken it as an invitation was obvious. Well, why not? They were engaged, could marry any time they felt like it, so why shouldn't they sleep together?

But she wasn't quite ready for that yet, and launched into a hurried conversation about how Rourke disapproved of non-caste people being on the set.

'Damn,' Harvey muttered. 'And I was looking forward to seeing him at work. The word is that he's a genius. And he's supposed to be marvellous with the people who work with him.'

'I'm sure he can't be any better than Jason,' she defended.

Her fiancé shrugged. 'Only time will tell.'

It would indeed! 'I think I should write to Jason, tell him how sorry I am that he's not able to be here.' Sorrier than anyone would ever know, she thought bitterly.

'I sent a telegram.'

Her eyes widened. 'You did? When?'

'As soon as I found out about the accident——'

'You could have said——'

'I told you, I forgot.'

'Yes,' she sighed. 'So what will you do while I'm working?'

Harvey shrugged. 'Look around Los Angeles, I suppose.'

She was glad to be spared that. At least this way Harvey would have no excuse to drag her off to see her mother. It might be years since she had been so disillusioned, but she still couldn't forget her mother's part in the past.

It was as if Harvey partly read her thoughts. 'I telephoned your mother this afternoon.' He looked at her warily.

Clare's mouth tightened. 'Why?'

He sighed. 'Because I had told her we would probably call round there this morning.'

'You had no right—I'm sorry,' she drew a controlling breath. 'But I really have no intention of seeing my mother while I'm here.'

'It's been years, Clare——'

'And it can be another ten for all I care! I'm sorry, Harvey, but about this I'm adamant. Now can we forget my mother?' She moved insinuatingly against him.

Harvey was nowhere near being immune to her body pressed against his. 'She's already forgotten,' he groaned as her hands became entangled in his hair. 'For now.'

That last irked her, but she pulled his head down to her, inviting his kiss, longing for forgetfulness. And perhaps in Harvey's arms she would finally find it.

He was breathing raggedly by the time they broke the kiss, murmuring his consent as she slid the jacket off his shoulders, slowly unbuttoning his shirt.

'Clare?' he questioned uncertainly.

'Don't ask questions, Harvey,' she groaned. 'Please. Just make love to me.'

He gasped as her fingertips ran the length of his bare chest. 'Are you sure?'

'Very,' she nodded, determination in her eyes.

He kissed her again, his hands moving caressingly over the thin material covering her breasts. 'How do I get this off?' he muttered after a few minutes of frustrated efforts to find the opening.

She kissed his throat and jaw, wishing he wouldn't talk so much. 'The buttons are at the back.'

It took some minutes, but he finally removed her blouse, his hands and mouth caressing her bared breasts. Clare lay back on the sofa, her eyes closed, wishing,

wishing—Oh *God*, she was wishing it were *Rourke*!

She sat up with a jerk, her eyes panic-stricken. She *couldn't* have been wishing it were Rourke making love to her, not after all this time. She couldn't!

'What is it, darling?' Harvey was flushed with desire, his hair dishevelled, his shirt unbuttoned to his waist.

Clare looked at him as if he were a stranger to her. 'I think you'd better go,' she said distantly. 'I—I'm too tired tonight.'

'Is that all it is?' He was frowning down at her, smoothing her tangled hair back from her face. 'You look very pale.'

She moved away from his caressing hand, sickened with herself, with the way she had been going to use him. 'I'm just tired.' She forced a wan smile to her lips. 'I'm sorry, darling.'

'That's all right,' he ruefully accepted her decision, helping her back into her blouse, patiently refastening all the tiny little pearl buttons down the back before buttoning his own shirt. 'Another night, hmm?'

She could have cried with the understanding way he accepted sexual disappointment. 'Thank you, Harvey,' there was an emotional catch in her voice as she clung to him. 'You're so good to me.'

'Don't be silly,' he chided gently. 'You're my fiancée, of course I'm good to you. Now I think you should get to bed—alone. Somerville won't be very pleased if you turn up with bags under your eyes tomorrow.'

Clare blushed as she remembered Rourke telling her to sleep alone tonight. How surprised he would be if he knew she never did anything else! 'I'll look my best,' she assured Harvey.

'You always do.' He stood up to leave. 'Call me to-morrow when you've finished for the day—I'll be in my room. How about breakfast, shall we have that to-gether?'

'I think I'll just have coffee in my room,' she smiled her refusal.

Once Harvey had left she went through to the bath-room to wash and change into her nightgown, putting her hair loosely on top of her head as she cleansed her face of make-up. She only ever wore a light make-up, just lip-gloss and a foundation, but she knew that with-out it she looked eighteen again—and just as vulner-able.

Harvey was right, she did look pale, and the brown lacy nightgown made her appear even more so. But it was a pretty gown, with ribbon shoulder-straps, lacy cups over her firm uptilted breasts, a silky sheath over the rest of her body to her ankles.

Her hands were up loosening her hair from the ribbon as she came back into the lounge area, arrested in the action as she saw Rourke Somerville sitting in one of the armchairs, one leg dangling over the side as he lounged down in the chair.

Her hands dropped down to her sides as she realised how tightly the material was pulled tautly across her breasts and firm outstanding nipples. 'What the hell are you doing in here?' she demanded indignantly, her eyes blazing.

His leg moved to the floor, and he sat forward in his seat, his gaze appreciative as it moved over her. 'Waiting for you,' he dryly stated the obvious.

'*How* did you get in here?' She was breathing heavily, Rourke's gaze fixed on her heaving breasts. But she couldn't help it, coming out here and finding Rourke in her sitting-room the last thing she had been expecting. It was a wonder she hadn't fainted with shock!

Rourke didn't say a word, instead he stood up, moving to the doors the porter had told her separated the Royal Suite into two separate suites, sliding the doors apart before looking back at her, his eyebrows raised meaningly.

Clare's eyes widened as she took in everything about the other room—the open script, the used tray from dinner still on the dining-table, the dark green shirt thrown on one of the chairs. Rourke had worn that shirt to the meeting this afternoon!

She swallowed hard. 'You—you're staying there?' Her voice came out as a squeak.

Rourke nodded. 'Convenient, isn't it?' he drawled.

She shot him a sharp look; convenient for what? She bit her lip, drawing in a deep controlling breath. 'You—you aren't staying at the beach-house, or the house in Bel Air?'

'I no longer have the house in Bel Air,' he told her. 'And no, I'm not staying at the beach-house.'

She clasped her hands together to hide their trembling. 'Why aren't you?'

He shrugged. 'I didn't want to commute every day.'

'But did you have to have the suite next to mine?' she groaned. This afternoon she had thought the nightmare couldn't get any worse—it just had!

'I am your co-star,' he taunted.

Her mouth set mutinously. 'Then I'll ask to be moved. I don't need a large suite like this anyway.'

Rourke's eyes hardened to blue chips of ice. 'You'll do no such thing.'

'I will——'

'No, you won't,' he told her in a controlled voice. 'What explanation would you give for the change?'

'I—Well, I—I——'

'Would you tell *darling* Harvey that you didn't want to be this close to your ex-lover?' he taunted.

Clare paled even more—if that were possible. 'You were listening . . .!' she gasped.

Rourke nodded, his mouth twisting. 'Every word, Clare *darling*,' he softly mocked.

'Then you heard—you heard——'

'You acting the part of a little tease again?' he asked in a bored voice. 'Yes, I heard. Your years at drama school have definitely paid off, Clare. It was a most convincing performance. You had poor Pryce almost apologising for desiring what you intended him to desire. You haven't changed, Clare,' he added contemptuously. 'And you still ask to be made love to very nicely.'

'Get out of here,' she choked, feeling sick. 'Just get out!'

'When I'm good and ready. In view of the fact that I can—er—hear everything that goes on in this room, perhaps it would be as well if you didn't entertain Pryce during your stay here.'

'We can always go to his room!' she said defiantly.

Sparks of anger flared in his eyes. 'You little bitch!' he rasped, taking a threatening step towards her.

Clare backed away. 'Don't you come near me,' she warned in a panic-stricken voice, terrified of what might happen if he touched her.

Rourke came to a halt, the contempt deepening in his eyes. 'I have no intention of coming near you. I'm still not the right man to try your teasing ways on. You haven't forgotten what happened last time you tried your advance and retreat routine on me?'

'No,' she answered through numbed lips, her head going back. 'But I thought you had.'

'I thought I had too,' he nodded grimly. 'But listening to you just now, with your *loving* fiancé, brought all the memories back.' He looked her over consideringly, almost insultingly. 'You're thinner than you were then, more haughty too——'

'I've grown up,' she corrected distantly.

His mouth twisted. 'You were always grown up, it just took me a while to realise *how* grown up. You should know by now, Clare, that you don't need to *ask* men to make love to you, they can't help themselves.'

Her eyes flashed as she looked at him angrily. 'Including you?' she taunted.

Rourke looked as if he would like to hit her. 'Including me?' he ground out.

'Couldn't you help yourself?' she said bitterly. 'No, of course,' she scorned. 'You completely lost control, didn't you? You couldn't even stop when you knew how much I hated it.'

His expression was savage, his mouth a thin, straight line, his hands clenched into fists at his sides, those hands that had eventually caressed her to abandonment. 'You don't hate it now,' he said contemptuously, his eyes leaving her in no doubt of his disgust. 'I guess you're Carlene Walters' daughter after all.'

Clare went deathly white, clutching at the back of a chair for support. 'I am nothing like my mother,' she choked. 'Absolutely nothing!'

'Aren't you?' he sneered.

'No!' she spat the word at him. 'But at least she had the sense to throw you out.' For months she had expected to see the announcement of her mother's marriage to this man, had lived in dread of having Rourke as her stepfather. But it had never materialised. There had been the much-publicised break-up of her mother's long-term romance with Perry, and then a series of reports of other boy-friends who filtered in and out of her mother's life, but Rourke's name was never mentioned.

'She didn't throw me out, Clare,' he answered coldly. 'I had the sense to walk out.'

'And are you going to walk out now? Or do I have to get Harvey back to throw you out?'

Rourke's mouth turned back in a sneer. 'He could try.'

He was right, in any show of strength between the two men Rourke would emerge the victor, still in the peak of physical fitness. 'Will you just leave?' she said wearily, her shoulders drooping in defeat. She had taken enough of a beating today, she wasn't sure how much more she could take.

'Yes, I'll leave.' He sauntered over to the connecting door. 'Don't forget you're expected in make-up at six-thirty.'

'I know that!' she snapped. 'And I won't be late,' she added defensively.

'I didn't think you would be,' he taunted. 'I was just reminding you. And I want you to have more than coffee for breakfast.'

'You really were listening!' she gasped.

He gave an arrogant inclination of his head. 'I already told you I was. I'm going to order breakfast for six o'clock, perhaps you would like to join me?' he mocked.

'No, thank you,' she snapped. 'Looking at you across the breakfast table is the one thing guaranteed to put me off my food,' she added childishly.

Rourke obviously thought it was too. 'Not worthy of you, Clare,' he shook his head. 'I felt sure you would have gained a little sophistication by now.'

'I don't need sophistication to know exactly what you are, Rourke Somerville,' she snapped with dislike, wounded by his scorn. 'If anything I dislike you even more than I did five years ago.'

His eyes narrowed to steely slits. 'Any time you feel like showing your—dislike, in the same way, just knock on the door. If I'm not busy at the time I just might oblige you.'

Before Clare could make any cutting remark in reply he had gone back into his own suite, sliding the doors back together, the catch falling back into place.

She switched the lights off, running into her bedroom and closing the door before the tears came, throwing herself down on the bed as she sobbed uncontrollably.

It hadn't occurred to her that Rourke would be staying on board the *Queen Mary* too, assuming that he would be staying in Hollywood. Knowing he was actually *next door* filled her with apprehension.

And it shouldn't! She had already decided he couldn't reach her. But he had, he had! His derision had been like a physical blow, and she blushed with humiliation to think he had heard her begging Harvey to make love to her. Thank God she hadn't actually gone through with it, with knowing that Rourke had heard that too.

Facing the fact that she had been imagining Harvey

was Rourke was even harder to bear. She had never
done that before, had never wanted to do that before,
and she couldn't understand why she had done it now.
Perhaps seeing Rourke again, having faced all the feelings, the longings she had once had for him had brought
that feeling on. She sincerely hoped that was the case.

Despite her pleas of tiredness it was the early hours
of the morning before she fell asleep, a deep drugged
sleep that was filled with nightmares she couldn't escape
from.

When she finally woke up she thought she must still
be in the middle of one, for Rourke stood at her bedside,
a cup in his hand.

'Your coffee,' he drawled. 'I took the liberty of having
two cups brought with my breakfast.'

This was no nightmare but the real flesh and blood
Rourke! She stared at him in blank astonishment, wondering how he managed to look so lithe and attractive
at—'What time is it?' she asked groggily.

'Just after six. Do you want the coffee or not?' he
thrust the cup at her.

'I—Yes, I want it.' Clare bit back the refusal, knowing
she wouldn't have time now to order any for herself,
and feeling desperately in need of some. She sat up,
pulling the sheet up to her chin, blushing as Rourke
openly mocked the action. 'At least you're more gentlemanly this morning,' she muttered irritably.

'I would have thought gentlemanly was the last thing
you wanted me to be last time,' he drawled.

She gave an impatient sigh and took the cup from
him, securing the sheet beneath her chin as she leant
back against the headboard to drink the coffee. It was
just as she liked it, plenty of milk and a dash of sugar.
She looked up at him questioningly after the first sip.

Rourke shrugged. 'I remembered.'

'Thank you,' she said primly 'And by gentlemanly I
was referring to last night, not—not——'

'Not five years ago.' He sat down on the stool in

Say Hello to Yesterday

Holly Weston had done it all alone.

She had raised her small son and worked her way up to features writer for a major newspaper. Still the bitterness of the the past seven years lingered.

She had been very young when she married Nick Falconer—but old enough to lose her heart completely when he left. Despite her success in her new life, her old one haunted her.

But it was over and done with—until an assignment in Greece brought her face to face with Nick, and all she was trying to forget. . . .

Time of the Temptres

The game must be played his way!

Rebellion against a cushioned, controlled life had landed Eve Tarrant in Africa. Now only the tough mercenary Wade O'Mara stood between her and possible death in the wild, revolution-torn jungle.

But the real danger was Wade himself—he had made Eve aware of herself as a woman.

"I saved your neck, so you feel you owe me something," Wade said. "But you don't owe me a thing, Eve. Get away from me." She knew she could make him lose his head if she tried. But that wouldn't solve anything. . . .

Your Romantic Adventure Starts Here.

Born Out of Love

It had to be coincidence!

Charlotte stared at the man through a mist of confusion. It was Logan. An older Logan, of course, but unmistakably the man who had ravaged her emotions and then abandoned her all those years ago.

She ought to feel angry. She ought to feel resentful and cheated. Instead, she was apprehensive—terrified at the complications he could create.

"We are not through, Charlotte," he told her flatly. "I sometimes think we haven't even begun."

Man's World

Kate was finished with love for good.

Kate's new boss, features editor Eliot Holman, might have devastating charms—but Kate couldn't care less, even if it was obvious that he was interested in her.

Everyone, including Eliot, though Kate was grieving over the loss of her husband, Toby. She kept it a carefully guarded secret just how cruelly Toby had treated her and how terrified she was of trusting men again.

But Eliot refused to leave her alone, which only served to infur ate her. He was no different from any other man... or was he?

These FOUR free Harlequin Presents novels allow you to enter the world of romance, love and desire. As a member of the Harlequin Home Subscription Plan, you can continue to experience all the moods of love. You'll be inspired by moments so real...so moving...you won't want them to end. So start your own Harlequin Presents adventure by returning the reply card below. <u>DO IT TODAY!</u>

front of the dressing-table area. 'It was five years ago,' wasn't it?'

'Yes,' she acknowledged tightly. 'Would you mind getting out of here while I shower and dress?'

He stood up, coming back to the bedside. 'Not at all. Finished with the cup?'

She hastily drank the last of it down, handing him the empty cup. 'Thank you.'

She shied away from noticing how handsome he looked in brown fitted trousers and shirt. No man should look this good first thing in the morning, especially when she was feeling so vulnerable having just woken up from dreaming about him.

'My pleasure.' Rourke put the cup down on the side. 'I have to make sure my leading lady is—happy.'

She looked up at him apprehensively, not liking the way he was looming over her. 'I am happy,' she said nervously.

'Are you?' he questioned huskily.

'Of course——'

'Then why were you so restless last night?' he asked shrewdly.

Clare paled. 'How do you know I was restless?'

'I came in and looked at you,' he stated calmly.

As quickly as the colour had left her cheeks it now flooded back. 'You came in here and looked at me?' she repeated disbelievingly.

'Yes,' he confirmed unconcernedly.

'You just walked in here——'

'Yes,' he repeated impatiently.

'You had no right——'

'The way you were yelling I thought someone was attacking you.'

Her mouth twisted. 'And I'm sure that bothered you.'

'Yes,' his eyes narrowed, 'as a matter of fact it did.'

'Why?' She pushed the bedclothes back, aware of the time passing even if Rourke wasn't, and swung her legs to the floor, pushing her hair away from her face.

Rourke was watching her every movement. 'Has anyone ever told you how good you look first thing in the morning? Of course they have,' he impatiently answered his own question. 'Well, I'm reinforcing that statement. You look—God, you look beautiful, Clare!'

She had no chance to move away as he lowered his body down on to hers, pushing her backwards as his mouth came down on hers.

To Clare it was as if the years were stripped away, her lips flowering beneath his, allowing him access to the moist warmth of her mouth. They were back in the beach-house, in Rourke's bedroom, in Rourke's bed—and once again she didn't want his caresses to stop.

His lips moved from her mouth to her throat as he slipped her shoulder straps down her arms, pulling the nightgown down to her waist, her breasts bared to him now. He slowly slid down her body, capturing the full, taut nipple into his mouth. His teeth gently bit, his lips seducing—and all the time Clare was making little whimpering noises of pleasure in the back of her throat.

Rourke knew her body so well, knew all the pleasure spots, removing the nightgown completely now as his lips caressed a trail of fire over the flatness of her stomach, lingering over the softness of her inner thigh.

Clare gasped her pleasure, arching against him, the wildfire excitement of her body telling her that she was ready for his possession, that she wanted him, *now*.

'Rourke,' she pulled his head up to her, raining heated kisses on his throat and jaw, the masculine smell of his aftershave and the more sensual male smell of his body acting like an aphrodisiac on her senses. 'Oh, Rourke . . .' she groaned as his lips once more claimed hers, becoming fiercer as his passion rose to meet hers, the whole length of his body lying on top of her now, the feel of his clothing pleasurably abrasive on her heated flesh.

He pushed his knee between hers, pushing her legs apart as he lowered himself down between her thighs.

Clare moaned in her throat at this more intimate contact, wanting all of him. 'Rourke, please——' she watched in dazed stupefication as he levered himself up and away from her, bereft at the loss of his body from hers. 'Rourke . . .?' She looked up at him with hurt eyes.

'Yes?' he asked tersely, his hands thrust into his trousers pockets stretching the material revealingly across his thighs, showing that he was still aroused.

She frowned her puzzlement, reaching out a hand to him. 'Why have you left me?' she choked, finding she was unable to cope with this sexual disappointment, her whole body seeming to ache with repressed emotion.

His mouth turned back in a sneer. 'You really don't know, do you?' he scorned.

She flinched as if he had hit her, feeling as if he had. 'No . . .' There was a wealth of pain in her voice.

'Do you use the same routine with every man you sleep with?'

'Routine . . .?' she gasped.

'Yes,' he rasped, looking at her contemptuously as she bent down to pull the sheet over her nakedness. 'Do you always ask in that way?'

'Ask . . .?' she blinked her bewilderment. 'I don't understand.'

He paced the room impatiently, shooting her disgusted glances. 'Maybe you just do it without realising it.'

'Do *what*?' she cried her frustration, wondering what she had done to suddenly change this man from a passionate lover to a furiously angry man.

'Beg, Clare,' he snapped harshly. 'You always *beg*! Five years ago you begged, last night with your fiancé you begged, and just now you begged again. Maybe you've just slept with so many men you don't even know you do it. And damned fools that they are, those men probably think it's *them* you really want. What is it, Clare?' he scorned savagely. 'Do we all look the same after a while?'

She was a sickly grey colour by this time. 'Get out of here. Get out!' her voice rose in hysteria.

'Oh, I'm going,' he sneered.

'And don't come through that connecting door again!' she shouted after him.

Rourke paused at the door. 'I'll come through there any damned time I feel like it,' he told her coldly.

'No!'

'Yes.'

'You—you can't,' she protested, desperation in her voice. 'What if Harvey should see you?'

'Ah yes, Harvey. Remembered him, have you?' he taunted scathingly. 'The man you're going to marry.'

'I never forgot him!' her eyes blazed at him. 'I just—I just——'

'You wanted me.' His mouth turned back. 'Well, sometimes it does us good to go without the things we want. I wanted you five years ago, but you ran away to England like the frightened little girl you were.'

'And we both know why!'

'Do we?' he said wearily. 'I didn't, not at the time.'

'I'm sure my mother told you!'

'Mm—eventually. Get dressed, Clare,' he said impatiently. 'It's almost six-thirty.'

She refused to get out of bed until he had gone. 'Make sure you close the connecting door,' she ordered angrily.

'I'll do that,' he nodded, quietly leaving the room.

Oh God, what had she done now?

CHAPTER SIX

CLARE hurried into the adjoining bathroom, not having much time to get ready if she wasn't going to get the reputation of being late. She didn't give herself time to think, to analyse what had happened this morning, knowing that to do so would only give her further pain.

She dressed in denims and a sun-top, applying no make-up, and brushing her hair up into a ponytail, knowing that once she reached Make-up and Wardrobe her whole appearance would be changed anyway. She hardly looked like someone from the 1950s at the moment!

Like most films she had worked on this one was being filmed out of sequence, the post-war scenes being filmed first, a lot of the pre-war scenes being shot in a studio, the *Queen Mary* having undergone a lot of changes since she had been painted grey and was known as the 'Grey Ghost' during the six war years when she had acted as a troopship to hundreds of thousands of soldiers.

Of course the shipping line had tried to return the ship to its former state, but some of the changes made had been irreversible, the initials of hundreds of soldiers scratched into the wood of the walls in the area now known as Piccadilly Circus being one of them. Most of the ship's walls had been covered to protect them, but the walls in this area were curved and almost impossible to cover. At the end of the war there had been thousands of soldiers' initials scratched into the woodwork, making it necessary to cover it with pseudo-leather. It seemed a shame to Clare, but then it was one of the smaller prices to pay for war, she supposed.

This film had appealed to her because it was a love story with a difference, the story of Lady Caroline

Hammond and Gunther Bernhardt, a well-do-to Englishwoman and a rich German industrialist. They had crossed the Atlantic together on the *Queen Mary*, but a couple of months after reaching New York, war had been declared between their two countries. It had been a war that had torn them apart, that had ripped their growing love asunder. Fifteen years later they were to meet again, also on the *Queen Mary*, but Lady Caroline was now married to a prominent English politician.

What Clare particularly liked about this story was the fact that Caroline and Gunther didn't do what everyone considered 'right', that this time they stayed together, in America, Caroline leaving her husband, Gunther leaving his beloved Germany. The story had depth, love—if only Rourke weren't to play Gunther!

She came up with a start when she saw Rourke was once again sitting in her lounge area. 'I thought I told you to get out,' she said stiffly.

'You did.' He slowly stood up, moving with a grace of movement that reminded Clare of a dangerous feline. 'And I got out of the bedroom. I also closed the connecting door,' he mocked.

She flushed. 'I meant *after* you,' she said resentfully, her emotions still churning from their earlier encounter.

'I know that,' he gave a taunting smile. 'But I thought if we both turned up late it wouldn't look so bad for you.'

Her eyes narrowed suspiciously. 'You did?'

'Mm,' he opened the door for her to leave. 'After all, I am the reason you're late.'

Colour flooded her cheeks as she was forced to remember the time she had spent with him on her bed. 'I don't want that to happen again,' she told him abruptly, her head held high as they walked down the deserted corridor; most of the other passengers were still sleeping.

Including Harvey! She had betrayed him this morning, had let him down in the worst way possible.

'I wouldn't if I were you,' Rourke drawled at her side.

She gave him a sharp look, her eyes shadowed. 'Wouldn't what?' she asked impatiently.

'Tell Harvey about this morning.'

She flushed her resentment of his ability to read her thoughts; she never knew what he was thinking, a mask always over his inner feelings. 'He has a right to know——'

'Does he?'

'Yes! Doesn't my engagement mean anything to you?' she snapped.

Rourke shrugged. 'About as much as it means to you—and judging by your reaction to me fifteen minutes ago, that isn't much.'

Clare stiffened. 'I happen to love—and respect—Harvey very much.'

He seemed unimpressed with her claim. 'Whatever you feel for him it obviously isn't enough, not for you. I can guarantee that within six months of the wedding you'll be looking round for someone new.'

'I won't!' She was indignant.

'You will,' he said with certainty. 'And just for the record, if it had been me last night and not your fiancé I would have taken you.'

She flushed. 'I know all about your brute force!'

'It wouldn't have been brute force,' he said harshly. 'I didn't hurt you this morning, did I?'

'No . . .'

His mouth twisted. 'I don't usually hurt my women when I make love to them.'

'Oh, I see,' she scorned. 'You just made me the exception.'

His face darkened ominously. 'I never meant to hurt you, and you know it. You should have told me——'

'That I was a virgin?' she said shrilly. 'And not the little film-star groupie you thought I was. To be paid for my services,' she added bitterly.

'Groupies don't usually get paid, they do it for the glamour,' he rasped. 'And the money I left you was for a cab, nothing else. God, I knew you were no groupie!'

'But you took me anyway.'

'You asked me to, damn you!' he said fiercely.

'So I did,' her tone was bitter. 'And I lived to regret it.'

'So did I,' Rourke muttered.

'What did you say?' she asked sharply.

'It wasn't important,' he dismissed bleakly.

He didn't need to repeat it, she knew exactly what he had said. Why did he regret it? Could it be that her mother had actually been angry about his seduction of her, that that was in fact the reason he and her mother had broken up? At the time her mother hadn't seemed at all concerned, and it had been this that had made Clare never want to see her again. But what if she had been wrong, what if her mother really had cared, had finished with Rourke on the basis of that?

'Maybe it's best that I kissed you this morning,' Rourke remarked dryly.

'I don't happen to think so,' she snapped.

He eyed her mockingly. 'But how would it have looked to the others if you'd reacted on set to me like that?' he drawled mockingly.

Colour flooded her cheeks. 'You caught me unawares this morning,' she told him coldly. 'It won't happen again.'

'Won't it?' he taunted.

'No!'

'If you say so,' he shrugged.

'I do.'

'I heard you quite clearly the first time,' he mocked her vehemence.

'As long as you realise I meant it.'

His mouth curled back into a mocking smile. 'Whatever happened to Little Miss Cool I heard so much about?'

Clare wondered briefly who he had heard that description from, although it wasn't so surprising, since the media often mentioned her coolness. Well, she wasn't cool now, and she hadn't been since meeting Rourke again.

'I'm still here,' she said tightly.

'I wonder,' he drawled.

Once her make-up was applied and she had on Lady Caroline's clothes, Clare forgot all about being anything but Lady Caroline. She might be disturbed by working this closely with Rourke, but no one could dispute her professionalism.

Except Rourke! Nothing she did was good enough for him, so much so that by lunch-time she felt quite awful.

'Whew!' Rena collapsed into the chair next to Clare's as they both ate a sandwich lunch and hot, strong coffee. The latter on Rourke's orders—he said they all needed waking up! 'He's being a bastard, isn't he?' she sighed.

Clare almost choked over her sandwich. The description was a little—colourful, even if it were true. She shrugged. 'He wants it done perfectly, I can understand that.'

'Oh, so can I,' Rena grimaced. 'But I haven't noticed him pointing out any of dear Belinda's faults.'

'Belinda Evans?' Clare frowned, glancing at the dark-haired actress who was playing the part of one of the other passengers on board. The other girl was petite and gaminely beautiful—and as Rena had pointed out, Rourke had had nothing but praise for her all morning. Clare hadn't noticed it at the time, but she realised it now.

'Maybe she's the latest, hmm?' Rena put into words what Clare had only been thinking.

'Maybe,' she agreed noncommittally, wondering why every conversation she had lately seemed to be about Rourke.

But she looked at Belinda with new eyes, noticed the way the other girl smiled coyly at Rourke, the way she touched him whenever she could. And Rourke didn't seem to mind in the least, rather he seemed to like it.

By the end of the day Clare was glad to get away; her temples were aching—and mainly due to Rourke's attentions to Belinda! And she hated herself for her jealousy.

How could she feel jealous about a man she despised, a man she had no respect for? She couldn't, she *wouldn't*.

'Dinner?' Harvey said cheerfully when he called for her at seven-thirty.

'Lovely!' She gave him a bright smile, already changed and ready to go. She had been aware of Rourke moving about his suite for the last hour, and she had no intention of giving him the privilege of listening to any more conversations between Harvey and herself.

Harvey smiled. 'I've booked a table at the Sir Winston.'

'How English!' she laughed as they moved out into the corridor, feeling protected with Harvey's arm about her waist, the open admiration in his eyes.

She wore a black dress, very revealing, her only jewellery a slender gold chain. As she had looked at herself in the mirror she had been reminded of the chunky gold chain and medallion that Rourke had worn five years ago, that he still wore. It had felt warm against her breasts this morning, a warmth obtained from the man himself. But Rourke was cold, cold and calculated, and she refused to think about him tonight.

Harvey tucked her hand solicitously into the crook of his arm. 'I believe Sir Winston Churchill travelled on the *Queen Mary* two or three times himself during the war.'

Her eyes widened. 'I didn't know that.'

'Mm,' he nodded. 'The initial D-Day invasion plans were made on board.'

Clare gave him a teasing look. 'I do believe you've swallowed the guide-book, Harvey!'

He gave her a sheepish grin. 'I didn't have anything to do this afternoon, so I took the tour round. It's very interesting.'

They went through to have a pre-dinner drink in the adjoining bar, seated at one of the tiny tables in the dimly lit room, a piano player softly serenading them.

'It makes you feel quite nostalgic, doesn't it?' Harvey said ruefully.

Clare pulled a face. 'I've been living in the past all day.'

'Rough, was it?' His hand covered hers as it rested on the table.

'A bit,' she nodded. 'Everyone was prepared to work with Jason, it's a little difficult to work with—someone else.'

He squeezed her hand sympathetically. 'Never mind, love. A good meal and you'll feel much better.'

The restaurant had pictures of Sir Winston Churchill all over its walls. They sat alone at a table near one of the windows in the main part of the restaurant, having walked through two smaller rooms to get here.

Harvey was right, a good meal inside her and she did feel better, more relaxed, enjoying the warm friendliness of the restaurant staff.

'Do you know why they originally had those orange mirrors installed?' Harvey asked once they had finished eating, alluding to the tinted mirrors on some of the walls.

There was open amusement in her eyes as she looked at him affectionately. 'More information from your tour?'

'Mm,' he gave a boyish grin. 'Well?'

'Tell me,' she encouraged, seeing that he was aching to tell her.

'Seasickness,' he announced.

Clare frowned. 'Seasickness?'

'Yes,' he nodded. 'If you were seasick on the voyage and you looked in one of the orange-tinted mirrors then you didn't look as ill as you felt.'

'Sneaky!' she laughed.

'I thought it was a clever idea.'

'Oh, it is,' she nodded. 'Maybe I should get one for the mornings,' she added teasingly.

Harvey gave her a reproachful look. 'You always look good, even first thing in the morning.'

She turned to look out of the window. They had a magnificent view of Long Beach and the lights of the town reflected on the water. It was beautiful, tranquil, utterly peaceful.

'Enjoy your meal?'

Her peace was shattered in that split second, and she spun round from her perusal of the harbour to see Rourke standing beside their table, his arm firmly about Belinda Evans' waist.

Harvey stood up politely. 'Somerville.'

'Pryce,' Rourke drawled. 'Belinda Evans,' he introduced the giggling actress at his side.

'Miss Evans,' Harvey nodded. 'I believe you know Clare.'

'Oh yes,' Belinda shot a triumphant smile in her direction.

Clare gave the other girl a startled look. Why was she looking at her like that? Oh God, she didn't know, she couldn't know . . .! She looked accusingly at Rourke, but he returned that look blandly.

'To answer your question, Mr Somerville,' Clare said slowly, her confidence returned; Rourke simply wasn't the sort of man to kiss and tell, 'the meal was first class. I can recommend the seafood.'

Belinda gave another giggle, and the sound grated on Clare's nerves, although Rourke seemed to find it attractive, smiling down indulgently at the other girl.

'No suggestive comments about seafood,' he warned Belinda in amusement.

The dark-haired actress smiled up at him. 'I was only going to say you certainly don't need to eat any of it,' she said throatily.

Clare's mouth tightened as Rourke gave a husky laugh. How could he fall for such blatant flirtation? It didn't need two guesses who was going to be sharing his bed tonight. Well, at least she wouldn't need to worry about him invading her suite!

She stood up. 'If you'll excuse us,' she said pointedly, 'we were just going through to the bar.'

Harvey looked surprised, but the emotion was instantly masked as he smiled at the other couple. 'Enjoy your meal.'

'Oh, we will,' Belinda laughed once again.

Clare could still hear that grating sound as she accepted the wine Harvey ordered for her in the bar, most of the tables full now, a steady hum of conversation and the soft piano playing masking their own conversation.

Harvey frowned at her. 'You really don't like him, do you?'

'Rourke?' she delayed. 'It isn't him I dislike,' she said in a distant voice. 'I just don't approve of directors dating the actresses working for them.' Heavens, how pompous she sounded! And how shocked Harvey would be if he knew the real reason for her disapproval.

He shrugged. 'I suppose it is a bit unethical.'

'Yes,' she agreed abruptly, wishing she had never mentioned it. It had been bitchy, and that was something she usually wasn't. At least, she hoped she wasn't.

'Is it upsetting you having Somerville playing Gunther?' Harvey asked concernedly.

It wasn't bothering her at all that Rourke was playing Gunther, he was even better in the role than Jason had been during rehearsals, and once she spoke the lines that were Caroline's then she became her, forgetting her own antipathy to Rourke for a while. No, it was having Rourke direct her that was upsetting her, his criticism, when directed at her, seeming to be ruthlessly cruel.

'Is it the nude scenes?' Harvey probed gently.

She swallowed hard. Oh God, the nude scenes! Not that it was full nudity, she drew the line at that, but she and Rourke would be in bed together, with both of them only wearing briefs. And a couple of those scenes were scheduled for next week!

Harvey could tell by her flushed face that she was indeed bothered by them. 'But I thought we'd talked all this out,' he said with infinite patience. 'A little nudity isn't going to hurt your career.'

She pulled a face. It had been going to be embarrassing enough with Jason, with Rourke it would be impossible. 'Doesn't it bother *you*, Harvey, as my fiancé?'

'Well, of course it does——'

'But?'

'But I can't see any real harm in it,' he shrugged. 'This film doesn't have a single word of smut in it, and the love scenes are beautifully written.'

'Yes, they are,' she agreed dully, wondering how on earth she was supposed to go through with telling Rourke, as Gunther, that she loved him. Five years ago it had been true of herself for Rourke—and she hadn't even had the nerve to say the words even then. 'Could we leave now, Harvey? It's been another long day.'

'Of course,' he agreed, holding back her chair for her.

As they left the bar and walked down the hallway to the door, Clare could see Rourke and Belinda just coming towards them. It was just her luck!

Rourke raised his eyebrows, his hand resting possessively on Belinda's elbow; the young actress was leaning all the more seductively against him, obviously having imbibed heavily during the course of their meal.

'Leaving?' Rourke drawled.

'Clare's tired,' Harvey explained politely.

'I *never* get tired,' Belinda put in brightly.

'How nice,' Clare said with exaggerated sweetness, giving Rourke a mocking look. He really had chosen himself a particularly stupid woman this time; Belinda acted even younger than her twenty years.

Belinda's eyes hardened as she saw that look. 'Maybe when I get older I'll tire more easily,' she answered with equal sweetness.

Clare refused to be drawn. Not even Belinda could call twenty-three old! The poor girl must feel very unsure of Rourke's affection. She knew the feeling! So it was to Rourke she directed her next barb.

'Maybe you should leave now, Mr Somerville, you must be exhausted.' She had to hold back a smile at the look of contrition on Belinda's face as she looked up at her escort. Rourke's expression was deliberately bland, although the glitter in his eyes as he looked at Clare showed he wasn't as unmoved as he appeared. 'If you'll excuse us?' she said to the other couple. 'Harvey?'

'Oh yes, of course.' His arm came about her waist. 'Goodnight.'

Rourke answered cordially enough, but Belinda didn't answer at all, and Clare could hear the other girl's throaty kittenish voice as she and Harvey left the restaurant. Poor Belinda, how she had jumped in with both feet!

'I'm not sure you were altogether kind,' Harvey remarked as they walked down the stairs to their deck.

'I'm not sure Belinda was either,' she replied lightly.

'Oh, I didn't mean that little cat,' he dismissed. 'She deserved everything she got.' He frowned. 'Although you'll have to watch out for that sort of professional jealousy, it could get nasty.'

Poor Harvey had no idea what Belinda's behaviour had all been about—and Clare hoped he never would know. She still had no idea how Belinda had guessed.

'No, I meant you weren't very polite to Rourke Somerville,' Harvey continued. 'After all, you have to work with him for several months, there's no point in antagonising him.'

She flushed her resentment of this criticism, even if it

was the truth. 'I'm sure Rourke took it in good stead,' she said stiffly. 'After all, I didn't say anything derogatory.'

'No . . .'

'Then let's forget it, Harvey. I'm sure they have.'

'Probably,' he agreed ruefully. 'Miss Evans seemed to have—other things on her mind.'

'I'm sure Rou—Mr Somerville does too,' she said waspishly.

'So do I.' He looked at her questioningly.

Clare's heart sank. 'I'm tired——'

'Of course you are,' he laughed. 'I'm really in no hurry, Clare,' he reassured her.

Why wasn't he? They had been engaged for months now, didn't he feel in the least impatient to force the issue of a physical relationship between them? Obviously not.

'Have you—Have there been many other women?' she asked as they walked along the deck, the evening, as usual, warm.

Harvey flushed. 'Really, Clare——'

'Really, Harvey,' she mocked gently. 'You're thirty-five, not fifteen.'

'My age has never bothered you before——'

'And it doesn't bother me now,' she smiled. 'I was just trying to point out that I realise that a man of your age must have had—some physical relationships.'

Harvey was obviously uncomfortable discussing such an intimate subject. 'I've never pretended otherwise—— '

'I'm not condemning, Harvey,' she laughed lightly. 'I'm just—curious.'

'Well, I lived with Shara, you know that,' he said reluctantly.

Clare stopped walking, moving to lean on the railing, looking out at Long Beach, the gentle breeze coming off the water ruffling her hair. She had known all about Harvey's live-in relationship with the girl he had managed before her, but it had never really interested her before. It did now.

She glanced sideways at Harvey. 'Why didn't you get married?'

He looked away. 'Shara wasn't interested in marriage.'

Her eyes widened. Somehow she had always thought it was Harvey who had opted out of the more permanent commitment of marriage. It came as something of a surprise to know that it was Shara Morgan who hadn't wanted that total commitment. She knew that the other woman was now starring in a popular American comedy show, although Harvey never mentioned her, or the success she had attained since coming to the States.

'Why?' Clare asked softly.

He leant on the rail beside her. 'She felt marriage would limit her career, especially if there were chileren.' He shrugged. 'I suppose she was right.'

'And have there been other women?'

He turned with a frown, irritation marking his brow. 'Why this sudden interest in my past sex life?'

She chewed on her top lip. 'I wondered what your opinion was on women who had—had other men,' she shrugged casually to take away the seriousness of the question.

'And have you?' he said quietly.

She paled. 'I—I wasn't talking about myself.'

'Weren't you?'

'No!'

'Clare . . .'

'I don't want to talk about it.' She spun away from him, not strolling now but walking determinedly to her room.

Harvey had joined her within seconds, his hand on her arm. 'I always knew there'd been someone else in your life, Clare,' he told her quietly.

She gave a visible start of surprise, but she didn't look at him, just continued walking. 'How did you know that?' she asked tightly.

'It was obvious,' he shrugged. 'When we first met you weren't interested in men, didn't even trust me,' he sounded slightly affronted. 'I knew you'd been hurt.'

'I——' she bit back the forceful denial. 'Yes,' she admitted softly, 'I was hurt.'

'And it involved your mother,' he said perceptively.

'I—Yes.'

'I thought so. But it was five years ago, Clare. And if your mother stopped you seeing the man then I'm sure she must have had good reason.'

'Oh, she did,' Clare agreed bitterly. 'She wanted him for herself.'

'Darling . . .?' Harvey looked taken aback.

She smiled at him. 'If you knew my mother you wouldn't find that so hard to believe.'

'But on the telephone——'

'You can hardly get to know someone on the telephone,' she derided.

'No . . .'

'So the fact that I—loved someone else, once, doesn't bother you?' she persisted.

'I'm not a prude, Clare.'

'No, but—Oh, never mind,' she dismissed. 'It isn't really important. If it doesn't bother you why should I let it bother me?'

The only trouble was that it did bother her! And it was still bothering her as she prepared for bed. Although why it should she had no idea, she had told Harvey as much as he needed to know. Maybe it was the fact that she had found it very hard to tell him and he hadn't really been interested that bothered her so much. It was different for a man, it was to be expected that he would have made love to other women, but Harvey hadn't even been interested in *who* his predecessor had been.

It was as she was climbing into bed that she heard the voices in the next suite, the slamming of the door—heavens, did they have no consideration for other people!—and Belinda's high-pitched giggle.

She was conscious of every sound, of the low murmur of voices, the chink of glasses. Lord, she wasn't to be subjected to Rourke making love to the other woman too, was she?

She couldn't bear it! If—It had gone quiet! Oh no, no, she wouldn't listen, couldn't hear the two of them . . .! She pulled the pillow over her head to block it out of her mind, but thoughts of Rourke and Belinda in bed together persisted.

She almost fell out of bed with surprise when the pillow was removed, and she saw Rourke looking down at her with mocking amusement.

'Having a bad dream?' he taunted.

Clare swallowed hard. 'Er—no. I—It was a bit noisy. I couldn't sleep.'

His eyebrows rose. 'Are you sure it wasn't a guilty conscience keeping you awake?'

Clare frowned. 'Guilty conscience?'

'Mm,' he nodded. 'For your bitchiness earlier.' His eyes hardened.

'*My* bitchiness?' She arched an eyebrow pointedly, and sat up in the bed, the pillow held defencively in front of her.

'Uh-huh,' he gave an inclination of his head. 'You were deliberately baiting Belinda.'

'I was not!' she denied heatedly.

'Then what would you call it?'

Her eyes flashed deeply gold. 'You have no right to come in here——'

'What would you call it, Clare?' he repeated coldly.

'*I* would call it your girl-friend's jealousy.'

Rourke's eyes narrowed. 'Of who?'

'Me!'

'You?' he frowned. 'Why the hell should Belinda be jealous of you?'

She flushed at the contempt in his voice. 'I don't know,' she snapped. 'Why don't we go into your bedroom and ask her?'

'My bed . . .? Really, Clare,' he taunted. 'And what would Belinda be doing in my bedroom?'

'The same as every other woman,' she said bitterly. 'Purring!'

His mouth hardened, his jaw inflexible. 'With the exception of one,' he rasped.

Clare's mouth twisted. 'There has to be the exception.' So her mother hadn't found him so satisfying after all! Maybe she really had misjudged her mother?

'Yes,' he said curtly. 'Well, I'm sorry to disappoint you, but Belinda is not in my bedroom.'

'Don't tell me you struck out?' she scorned.

'Belinda happens to be the daughter of an old friend——'

'My God, do you make a habit of it!'

'No! Belinda's *father* happens to be an old friend.' His eyes glittered dangerously. 'I told him I would keep an eye on her.'

'I'm sure he didn't expect you to keep *that* close an eye,' Clare mocked.

Rourke gave an impatient sigh. 'Will you let me finish talking, woman! Belinda is a little—wild——'

'How nice for you!'

'Will you shut up!' He stood up to pace the room, glowering down at her. 'She tends to get in with the wrong people——'

'She certainly did this time!'

'I'm warning you, Clare——'

'You aren't warning me anything, Rourke!' Her eyes sent out sparks. 'And if you don't stop using that connecting door I shall ask for a different suite, speculation or no speculation.'

'You knew I'd want to talk to you.'

'Tomorrow, perhaps,' she acknowledged, knowing that glitter in his eyes earlier had promised retribution. 'I don't expect you to keep walking in and out of my suite as if it were your own.'

'Point taken,' he nodded tersely.

Clare looked up in bewilderment. 'It is?'

A reluctant smile lightened his features. 'Don't look so surprised. I can be reasoned with—sometimes.'

'You surprise me,' she said dryly.

'I said sometimes, Clare,' he warned darkly.

'Sorry,' she muttered. 'So Belinda isn't in your bedroom?'

'No, and she isn't going to be. Would it bother you if she had been?'

Bother her? She had been suffering agonies imagining the two of them together!

'Of course not,' she denied coldly. 'Why should you think it would?'

His eyes were narrowed. 'Maybe because of this morning.'

'Nothing happened this morning,' she denied stiffly.

Rourke shook his head. 'How do you do it, Clare? How do you still manage to blush?' he explained at her questioning look.

'A good drama school,' she snapped, glaring at him.

'It must have been,' he muttered.

'It was!'

'Well, it wasn't good enough,' he rasped. 'Filming went badly today, you know that, don't you?'

'Do I?'

'You know you do,' Rourke sighed. 'You also know why.'

'I do?'

'Yes,' he snapped. 'It was because of you,'

Clare swallowed hard, looking down as her fingers plucked nervously at the pillow she still hugged. 'Me?' She bit her top lip.

Rourke resumed his pacing. 'You're as stiff as a board in every scene you have to do with me. I thought this morning might have cleared all that up——'

'I'm perfectly well aware of the reason you kissed me,' she choked.

'You don't know a damned thing!' he dismissed angrily. 'And I'm in no mood to tell you. Now I know you can act, I've seen the movies you've made, and you're good. But around me you freeze.'

How could she explain that with each moment she had to spend in his company she became aware of how much she still loved him? She had tried to deny it, even to herself, but seeing him with Belinda this evening had stripped away every barrier she had built up against him. She still loved Rourke Somerville, not even five years of not seeing him had changed that. Just as it hadn't changed the fact that he was still the biggest rake in Los Angeles. And if he thought for a minute that she believed that story of Belinda being the daughter of an old friend then he was mistaken! She knew him too well herself for that.

'I'm sorry,' she said stiffly. 'I'll try to do better to-morrow.'

'I hope so, because when I agreed to step into Jason's shoes and do this movie I was promised it would be completed in four months, the filming at least.'

'Four months?' Her eyes widened. 'Isn't that a little rushed?'

'It shouldn't be, you all had plenty of rehearsals in London before coming here.'

'But that was with Jason.'

Rourke shrugged, looking lean and relaxed in a dark dinner suit, the tie discarded at some time, the top two buttons of his white shirt now undone, the gold medallion nestling in the dark hair on his chest. 'It shouldn't be so different with me.'

Maybe it shouldn't be, but it was, for her at least. 'Your medallion,' she went off at a tangent, staring at it almost desperately as she shied probing the reason it was different with Rourke. 'Why do you wear it all the time?'

He frowned his annoyance. 'Clare——'

'I'd like to know,' she insisted shakily.

He grimaced. 'I bought it with the first fee I ever received for doing a movie,' he sighed. 'Satisfied?'

'It means a lot to you, doesn't it?'

'Yes, it means a lot to me! It means I showed that rich bitch of a mother of mine that I could make it without her, that I've never needed her or her money.'

Clare hadn't realised his bitterness went so deep—or that the medallion represented independence to him. It somehow made him seem as vulnerable as other mortals.

'Can we get on with discussing this problem now?' he said tersely.

'Problem?' she blinked. 'What problem?'

'You!'

'Oh—oh yes.' She chewed her bottom lip. 'I don't see what I can do about it. I just—I don't like working with you.'

'Because of the past?'

Delicate colour tinged her cheeks. 'Yes,' she sighed.

'Then forget about it.'

'Forget——?' Her eyes widened. 'How can I do that?'

'It should be quite easy. It meant nothing to you, so why not forget it? If you don't we'll never finish the movie. I've never turned in anything but my best, not in acting or directing, and I don't intend this to be the exception.'

'I told you, I can't help it!'

'You're going to ruin the whole movie with your frigidness.'

As quickly as she had blushed Clare now paled. 'I am not frigid!'

'Not you personally, just you acting,' he corrected tersely.

'For God's sake, Rourke, it was only the first day! Give it a chance.'

He ran one hand through his already tousled black hair, cut shorter earlier in the day to be in keeping with the part of Gunther. If anything he just looked more attractive, the shorter style drawing more emphasis to the ruggedness of his face and the mesmerism of his deep blue eyes.

'Okay,' he nodded. 'I'll give it until the end of the week.'

'And then what?' she asked wearily.

'I don't know yet. I'll think of something.'

Like he had thought of kissing her this morning! 'I'm sure you will,' she derided.

His eyes became cold. 'I mean to have this movie finished on time, Clare, with or without your co-operation. I have to be somewhere else in four or five months.'

'Your other film?'

'Yes.'

'What is it?' she asked interestedly.

'*Gun Serenade*,' he revealed reluctantly.

'I—But—That's my mother's next film!' She had seen reports of the film to be made of a South American revolution, and the Englishwoman who got caught up in it. She had also seen that her mother was to star in it. 'I didn't know you were the director,' she said dully.

'Well, I am. Unfortunately the place we'd picked out for filming has had its own revolution,' he explained dryly. 'The new government has given us permission to go in in four months. Too many arrangements had been made for us to change location, so we're waiting the four months. At least some of the filming should be lifelike!'

'But won't it—won't it be dangerous?'

'Don't worry, Clare,' his mouth twisted. 'Your mother will have all the security she needs. After all, she's still the Queen of Hollywood!'

Clare couldn't give a damn about her mother's safety, she was more interested in Rourke's safety—and with wondering if her mother's night security would consist of Rourke himself!

CHAPTER SEVEN

CLARE woke in the morning feeling physically sick, the nightmares so vivid, the bullets ripping into Rourke's body taking him away from her for ever. Reality was just as horrific—her mother and Rourke back together. Because it would be as inevitable as night following day.

The possibility of having Rourke as a stepfather loomed up once again, and she knew she couldn't stand it.

He had left her last night after assuring her that her mother would be well looked after, little knowing how little that bothered her, and she had heard the door lock behind him, evidence that he had taken notice of her complaint about him entering and leaving her suite whenever he felt like it.

Her night had been full of dreams of Rourke in danger, so much so that she didn't feel in the least rested, and moved listlessly about her suite getting herself ready.

When the knock sounded on her door she gave a start of surprise, her senses numbed from lack of sleep. She opened the door to find the corridor empty. If someone was playing a joke on her they had picked the wrong day!

The knock sounded again as she closed the outer door, and she moved to the communicating door. 'Rourke?' she queried tentatively.

'Who else were you expecting?' he drawled.

'What do you want?' she asked irritably.

'It isn't a question of what I want, but what you want.'

'Me?' she echoed sharply. 'I told you last night——'

'Coffee, Clare,' he taunted. 'I have a cup of coffee here for you.'

Her mouth set angrily, the aroma of strong coffee now reaching her. 'Open the door, then,' she instructed curtly.

Rourke did so, handing her the coffee. 'I asked Room Service if you'd ordered any, when they said no I ordered it with mine.'

Clare gave him an angry glare, determined not to notice how handsome he looked in tight denims and a blue sweat-shirt. 'I'm sure Room Service found that very interesting,' she snapped, turning away to drink her coffee, her own denims as tight as his, her tee-shirt body-hugging too.

'You look like hell——'

'Thank you!' she bit out angrily. 'That's just what I wanted to hear.' She knew she looked 'like hell'—she had looked in the mirror this morning! She was very pale, with dark shadows under her eyes. And it was this man's fault!

Rourke shrugged, leaning against one of the communicating doors. 'I can only tell you what I see.'

She shot him a resentful glance. 'You don't look too good yourself.'

He ran a hand around the back of his neck, rubbing his nape as if it ached. 'I didn't sleep too well.'

'Neither did I.'

'Frustrated, Clare?' he quirked a mocking eyebrow.

If it were possible she became even paler. 'What do you mean?'

His mouth twisted knowingly. 'Well, you've been without Pryce for two nights now. Maybe you have withdrawal symptoms.'

She slammed the cup down on the table, glad that it was empty, otherwise she would have got soaked! Her body was tense as she glared at him. 'For your information, Harvey and I do not sleep together,' she bit out fiercely. 'So I'm hardly likely to be feeling "withdrawal symptoms"!'

Rourke's eyes narrowed as they moved searchingly over her face, seeing the fury in her eyes, the anger in her mouth. 'You don't?' he said slowly.

'No,' she sighed. Oh dear, she had told him the one thing she had intended not to! And all because her defences were down after spending a night worrying about him.

She couldn't understand herself. She had spent five years *not* thinking about him, five years when he could have been involved in heaven knows what, could have been killed a hundred times, and yet within two days of seeing him again she was worrying about his welfare so much it was keeping her awake at night.

'Why don't you?' he pursued relentlessly.

She flushed. 'Harvey respects me——'

'Not that one, Clare,' he derided, shaking his head. 'Have you *ever* slept with him?'

'No.'

'What did you say?' he probed her muttered response.

'I said *no!*' she shouted. 'Now will you get out of here? I have to finish getting ready.'

'Why don't you?' he persisted on the subject of Harvey.

Her eyes sent out sparks at him. 'Mainly because we don't happen to be married.'

'I don't remember that bothering you with me,' Rourke derided.

'You're right, it didn't!' she almost spat the words at him. 'And it was my—experience with you that soured men for me.'

'You mean all this time . . .?'

'Yes, I mean all this time!' She was furiously angry, no longer caring what she said, what she revealed, not even noticing how pale Rourke had become. 'But that's going to change in the near future,' she declared with bravado. 'Why should I let one—disastrous experience ruin my whole life? Harvey is good and kind, and I'd rather have him as a lover than you any day.' Her breath was coming in gasps at the end of this tirade, her breasts heaving.

'The hell you would!' Rourke exploded, coming forward with angry strides to grasp her upper arms and pull her ruthlessly against him.

The force of her body meeting his knocked all the breath out of her body, rendering her momentarily helpless as his mouth came down to grind against hers, intending to give pain, not pleasure.

Rourke's complete disregard for her feelings caused the most pain, and she fought against him the whole of the time his mouth plundered hers.

At last she managed to wrench her mouth away from his. 'I hate you!' she told him vehemently. 'I hate you, damn you!'

He pushed her away from him with a disgusted sigh, whether with her or himself she couldn't tell, and ran a hand through his hair, ruffling the short dark curls. 'I'm sorry,' he said tightly. 'I didn't mean for that to happen.'

Clare wiped her mouth across the back of her hand. 'That's the trouble, you never do.'

He looked at her furiously. 'I have control. It's just that where you're concerned——'

'You don't,' she finished sneeringly. 'Well, I do. And I don't want you bringing me coffee any more, I don't want you coming in here any more, I just want you to stay away from me!'

'I get the message.' His mouth twisted. 'And don't worry, I don't want to be near you either.'

After an ugly argument like that it wasn't surprising that every scene they had to be in together was a total disaster—so much so that Rourke finally cancelled all their scenes together for the rest of the week.

'I can cope,' Clare claimed when she heard the news.

'Maybe you can,' Rourke muttered, 'but I can't. Now get out of my sight.'

'Rourke——'

'Yes, come on, Belinda,' he spoke to the other girl as she came on to the set, totally ignoring Clare as she still stood at his side. 'I'll help you with the lines,' he soothed the other girl. 'I realise this scene has come before you're ready for it, but Miss Anderson isn't quite up to her part yet.'

Clare knew that the last was meant as a direct dig at her, and Rourke's cruelty and Belinda's catty smile made her so angry she walked out, still in her costume, uncaring of the strange looks she received as she hurried to her suite.

Rourke had been cruel, deliberately so. The ruination of this morning's filming was not completely her fault. He had been as much still Rourke Somerville as she had been Clare Anderson, and their antipathy had taken over Gunther and Caroline, making the whole thing a farce. Rourke had been right to call a halt to it, but not to put all the blame on her.

She wouldn't cry, she refused to cry. She had shed too many tears over Rourke in the past, she simply didn't have any left where he was concerned.

A call to Harvey's room showed that he had already left for the day, leaving her free to do what she wanted. The trouble was she had no idea what she wanted to do. She hadn't wanted to go into Los Angeles during her stay here, but she refused to just sit in her room like a naughty schoolgirl.

She stood up with new impetus and took off her costume, taking care to hang it up properly—she wasn't feeling so courageous that she wanted to incur Rourke's wrath for a second time today. She had left her own clothes in the temporary wardrobe that had been erected on board, so she took out a pair of white tailored slacks, putting on a white silk blouse with them, brushing her hair loose about her shoulders, picking up her handbag and the keys to the car that had been put at her disposal for her stay here, then leaving the suite with a determined spring to her step.

Where she was going she had no idea, but she wanted to give the impression that she knew *exactly* where she was going, not wanting to get waylaid by anyone on her way out.

She didn't, sliding smoothly into the low red sports car, driving off with a roar of the engine. She hadn't driven in the States for years, and yet it seemed like yesterday; driving on the right-hand side of the road seemed perfectly natural to her.

The traffic was mad, as usual, but no madder than London during the rush-hour, and she seemed to be driving automatically, finding herself at Malibu Beach.

It was crowded as usual, mainly with fair-haired teen-agers all wearing the minimum of clothing. Clare got out of the car and moved forward to lean back against the bonnet, watching the antics of the laughing groups on the beach.

They all looked so happy, as she used to, and she wished she could return once again to those happy care-free days before she met Rourke. Then she had lived in ignorance of her mother's greed for every man to be interested in her, only in her, had been happy in a way she never expected to be again.

'Buy you a Coke, lady?'

'I—Gene!' she cried her recognition of the man who stood before her, the cut-off denims and tanned body so achingly familiar. 'Gene Lester . . .!' she said wonderingly.

'None other,' he grinned. 'Don't old friends get a welcome any more?'

'Of course they do!' She hugged him, still looking at him with disbelief. 'I can't believe this,' she laughed breathlessly.

'Neither can I,' Gene laughed too. 'My, you look good, Clare,' he looked her over appreciatively.

She gave a mischievous smile, feeling suddenly happy, lightheartedly so. 'You don't look so bad yourself.'

'And that from the girl who walked out on me without a word five years ago!' He gave a mock groan. 'I was yours for the taking, and here I am, still a bachelor.'

'You are?' she teased.

'I am.' He put his arm about her shoulders. 'Now how about that Coke?'

'Lovely!'

Clare took off her shoes as they walked along the beach, feeling as if she belonged now that she was with Gene, and not just an outsider looking in as she had done minutes earlier.

'Why did you disappear so suddenly five years ago?' Gene asked quietly.

She didn't even flinch, she had been expecting it. 'I didn't "suddenly" disappear, I went to England. I got a place in a drama school there.'

'Bit sudden, wasn't it?' He eyed her questioningly, not fooled for a minute.

She shrugged. 'Not really. It was what I wanted.'

'Funny, I thought it was Rourke you wanted.'

She licked lips that had suddenly gone dry. 'Rourke?' she delayed.

'I'm not fooled for a minute, sweetheart,' he chided. 'There's only one man in Hollywood called Rourke. And five years ago you were dating him, pretty heavily.'

'I was also dating you,' she reminded him.

'Not for two weeks before you left,' Gene shook his head.

Clare could see the direction they were heading, could see the familiar beach-house, and she didn't want to go there. 'Let's turn back now,' she suggested brightly.

'So that's Rourke's place.' Gene also looked at the beach-house. 'I knew he had one along here.'

She turned determinedly, giving an inward sigh of relief as Gene followed her. 'Yes, that's it.'

'Bad memories?'

'No, good ones,' she said dully. 'At least, they were good for me.'

'But not for Rourke.'

'Really, Gene,' she was once again lightly teasing, 'you seem obsessed with the man,' she dismissed. 'Now, tell me, how is life treating you?'

'I can't complain,' he shrugged.

'What are you doing now?'

'As little as possible,' he grinned.

She laughed. 'That sounds like you!'

He pretended to be insulted by her humour. 'I'll have you know I'm a valued man with a camera—a movie camera.'

'Why, Gene, I didn't know that. Congratulations. But if you're such a valued man,' she added teasingly, 'what are you doing loafing about on Malibu Beach?'

'Like I told you, as little as possible.'

'Seriously, Gene,' she chided.

He shrugged. 'The film I was due to be working on has been cancelled for a few months.'

'Don't tell me,' she grimaced, joining him down on the sand, sitting cross-legged beside him. *'Gun Serenade?'*

'Yes. But how did you——'

'Rourke is directing the film I'm in at the moment,' she explained reluctantly.

Gene's eyes widened in surprise. 'He is?'

'Mm,' she nodded.

'So that's where he is,' he said thoughtfully.

'Yes,' she laughed, but it was a laugh without humour. 'How is your father?'

'The same as ever. Oh, he's married again,' he added as an afterthought.

'He is?' Clare's eyes widened.

'Mm,' Gene grinned. 'I think he had a brainstorm— Lucy is only five years older than me.'

'Is she nice?'

'Very.'

'I'm glad.' She had always liked Perry, he deserved to be happy.

'Your mother and my father broke up years ago,' he supplied.

'Yes.'

'So,' Gene said briskly, 'who's the lucky man to put that ring on your finger?'

Clare felt on safer ground talking about Harvey, and blushed as she realised how much she was talking about him. 'Sorry,' she said ruefully.

'You're very fond of him, hmm?'

'Very,' she nodded. 'And you—is there a special girl in your life?'

'Not at the moment,' he shrugged.

'Still playing the field?' she teased.

'You could say that,' he drawled. 'Did you bring your bikini with you? We could go for a swim.'

'No, I didn't,' she said regretfully. 'I only came out for a drive.'

'Rourke gives you days off, does he?' he quirked one blond eyebrow.

'He—he didn't need me today,' she evaded.

'How does it feel to be a big star?' Gene teased.

'I don't know,' she smiled. 'I'll let you know if I ever become one.'

'From what I've heard you've already made it. One of these days you'll be invited to put your mark outside Mann's Chinese Theater.'

Clare knew this distinction was only enjoyed by about a hundred and fifty actors and actresses—and she doubted she could ever add to their number. 'One member of the family is enough,' she dismissed.

'Of course, your mother,' he nodded. 'How is she nowadays?'

Her expression became shuttered, her arms clasped about her bent knees as she gazed out across the water. 'I have no idea,' she said stiffly.

'You don't see her?' Gene seemed surprised.

'No.'

'I didn't know that,' he shook his head. 'Did it have anything to do with Rourke?'

'You knew, didn't you?' Clare was suddenly remembering another conversation she had had with Gene when he had warned her against getting involved with Rourke. 'You knew all the time,' she realised.

'About your mother's interest in Rourke? Yes,' he sighed. 'I think the whole of Hollywood knew.'

'Except me,' she recalled bitterly.

'Except you,' Gene nodded. 'You got hurt badly, didn't you?'

'At the time I did,' she dismissed tightly. 'But I'm over it now.'

'Are you?'

'Of course,' she flushed. 'I'm engaged to Harvey, we're getting married soon.' It was a slight exaggeration, since she had no idea when she and Harvey were getting married, but she felt she needed the added protection in front of Gene. He had always been too astute where she was concerned. 'Maybe you would like to come over one evening and meet him?' she invited warmly.

'Come over where?' he mocked.

'Sorry!' she smiled. 'We're staying on the *Queen Mary*.'

'In that case I'd love to come. She's been there for years now, but somehow I've never got to see her. Maybe I'll come early and take the tour.'

'I think all men are boys at heart,' she said ruefully. 'The tour was the first thing Harvey did when we got here,' she explained.

Gene laughed. 'We all like to imagine what it would have been like to be the Captain of such a ship.'

'It still has a Captain, so why don't you ask him?'

He shook his head. 'I didn't know that.'

'Harvey and I met him last night at dinner. Captain John Gregory,' she supplied, having liked the friendly man who had been introduced to them the previous evening in the Sir Winston Restaurant, finding him absolutely charming.

'It's a nice touch,' Gene nodded. 'But I suppose he's just a figurehead, only there for the tourists.'

'I don't think so,' Clare disagreed. 'From what I understand from the staff he's still the ultimate command.'

'Interesting job. Well, when do you want me to come to dinner?'

'I don't remember asking you to dinner,' she teased. 'Just for the evening.'

'If you aren't going to feed me I'm not coming.'

'Okay,' she laughed, 'I'll treat you to dinner. How about tomorrow?'

'Great,' he nodded agreement.

'No previous engagements?' she quirked an eyebrow.

'If I had I'd cancel it, for you.'

'You always were a flirt,' she chuckled, putting her shoes back on as they reached the road.

'I never flirt,' Gene complained. 'You just never take me seriously—you never did. I must have asked you to marry me fifty times in the past.'

'And you would have run a mile if I'd said yes.' She wiped the sand from her hands.

'Probably,' he admitted ruefully. 'Okay, I'll see you tomorrow some time.'

Clare hugged him. 'It's lovely to see you again, Gene—especially today. I—I was feeling a bit—down.'

He nodded. 'You looked it. Still, look at it this way, Clare, it can't last for ever.'

She blinked up at him. 'What can't?'

'Working with Rourke.'

She flushed. 'I'm not down because of working with Rourke.'

'Of course you aren't.' Gene held her car door open for her.

'I'm not!' She slid in behind the wheel.

'I agreed with you, didn't I?' he said with exaggerated innocence.

She gave him a look of irritation. 'It was the *way* you agreed.'

He gave her a wide-eyed look. 'You imagined it, Clare.'

'I'm sure!' she scorned, flicking on the ignition. 'I'll see you tomorrow. And, Gene, please don't mention my knowing Rourke to Harvey, he doesn't know we—knew each other in the past.'

'"Knew" in the full meaning of the word?' he quirked a questioning eyebrow.

'Mind your own business!' she snapped.

His mocking laughter followed her as she reversed on to the road. Maybe she had been wrong to invite him on to the ship, to meet Harvey. Gene was a mischiefmaker, and she wasn't sure she could trust him as regards mentioning Rourke and herself to Harvey.

Oh well, it was too late now. She would just have to make the best of it. And it had been nice seeing Gene again, had taken her back to the happy times.

It was almost dinner time by the time she parked the car in the car park next to the ship and walked over to the hotel, unknowingly graceful in her fitted white outfit. For the first time she noticed one of the many English telephone boxes in this area. They were the wrong colour! In England the telephone boxes, like the buses in London, were red, these were orange. She shrugged; not everything was perfect, after all.

Harvey wasn't in his room, Clare went back to the main desk to see if he had left a message for her. He hadn't. It wasn't like Harvey to just go off and not leave her word where he had gone.

There was a worried frown marring her brow as she let herself into her suite. She didn't know why she was surprised to see Rourke lounging on her sofa, but somehow she was. And he was asleep!

He looked more vulnerable in sleep, younger too, with no lines of cynicism to add the years. For long, timeless minutes she just drank her fill of him, knowing that as soon as he was awake the antagonism would be back, the anger they had for each other.

How she wished she could lie down beside him, could draw him into her, could once again know his full possession, be close to him.

She slammed the door hard behind her with the intimacy of her thoughts, coming fully into the room, her mouth twisting with satisfaction as Rourke gave a start and came awake with a jerk, blinking dazedly as he became aware of his surroundings.

Clare threw her handbag and keys down on the table. 'Comfortable?' she asked sarcastically.

'Not very.' He straightened, obviously still a little dazed. 'What time is it?' he asked groggily.

'Seven-thirty,' she answered abruptly. 'What are you doing in my room after saying you wouldn't invade my privacy again?' she demanded to know.

Rourke swung his legs down off the coffee-table. 'I'm damn well waiting for you! Where the hell have you been?'

She got herself a drink of water from the bathroom, feeling suddenly thirsty. 'Out,' she supplied curtly. 'Now I want to change for dinner——'

Rourke stood up, completely in control now, towering over her ominously. '*Where* have you been, Clare?' he repeated, dangerously soft.

'I told you——'

'*Where?*'

She flinched at the anger he conveyed in that one word. 'I went to the beach——'

'Malibu?' His eyes were narrowed.

'Yes,' she confirmed resentfully.

'You actually went to the *beach*?' His eyes glittered dangerously now.

'I—Yes.'

'Do you know I've been worried out of my mind about you?' He shook her roughly, glaring down at her.

'A-about m-me?' Clare felt as if her teeth were being rattled out of her head!

'Of course about you!' His fingers bit painfully into her shoulders, with little regard for the way she winced. 'I was a bit rough on you earlier——'

'Rough!' she found the strength to scorn. 'You were downright nasty!'

'I know that.' He thrust her away from him. 'I have no excuse——'

'I'm sure you don't!'

'Except that you're driving me insane!' he groaned, looking at her with tortured eyes. 'I don't find it any easier working with you than you do with me.'

'Where's your professionalism?' *She* was driving *him* insane! What on earth did he mean?

'Where's yours?' he derided.

She sighed. 'This situation is impossible. If I'd known—if I'd guessed you were going to be here I would never have come.'

'Strange, I had the opposite reaction. By the way, I have a message for you from Harvey.'

Clare was frowning. 'What do you mean, the opposite reaction?' He couldn't possibly mean what she thought he meant—could he? No, of course he couldn't! It was merely wishful thinking on her part.

Rourke raised one dark eyebrow. 'Don't you want to hear the message from Harvey?'

'I suppose so. I just——'

'You only *suppose* so? Shame on you, Clare,' he taunted.

'All right.' Her mouth set angrily, as she decided she must have imagined that look of desperation in his eyes seconds earlier. 'What did Harvey want me to know?'

'Apparently he's been delayed on business——'

'Business?' she echoed in a puzzled voice.

'That's what he said,' Rourke shrugged.

'Maybe he's made contact with someone at one of the studios—What he *said*?' she realised sharply. 'You mean you actually spoke to Harvey yourself?'

He looked at her steadily. 'Is there any reason why I shouldn't have done?'

She turned away, trying to digest what he was telling her. 'No, of course not. I just—How did you speak to him?'

'I just picked up the telephone when it rang and there he was,' Rourke derided.

Clare was still puzzled. 'Harvey rang you? But why would he do that? Unless of course he——'

'I picked up your telephone, Clare,' he put in softly.

Her eyes widened. '*My* telephone?'

'Mm,' he nodded unconcernedly.

'You came in here and answered *my* telephone?' she repeated indignantly.

'Any reason why I shouldn't?'

'You know damn well there is! What on earth will Harvey think?' she groaned.

'The truth, I suppose. That I heard your telephone ringing and answered it,' Rourke taunted her.

'But he doesn't know you're next door,' she said in exasperation.

Rourke frowned. 'Why doesn't he?'

'He just doesn't,' she muttered.

'It isn't a secret, is it?' he proved softly.

'Maybe if you didn't keep just walking in here I might have—mentioned it.' She was becoming more and more agitated by the minute.

'Well, he knows now,' Rourke shrugged.

'Yes, he does, doesn't he,' she said irritably. 'Heavens, I hate to think what construction he's going to put on this.'

'Doesn't he trust you?'

'Of course!' Her indignation rose.

'Then you have nothing to worry about, do you?'

'Of course I have something to worry about,' she snapped. 'If the roles were reversed, and a strange woman picked up Harvey's telephone when I called him, then I would demand a full explanation.'

'Then you don't trust him,' Rourke said simply.

'I do——'

'You can't, not if he would need to explain himself. Loving is trusting, Clare.'

'And what would you know about it?' she scorned. 'You've never loved anyone in your life.'

'And how do you know that?' His eyes were narrowed ominously.

'I just know,' she said bitterly. 'Now if you wouldn't mind leaving, I would like to change for dinner.' Perhaps she could join Rena and some of the others—she had heard them discussing meeting in the restaurant tonight.

'I—God, I just don't believe this!' Rourke grimaced. 'I came to see you to apologise and we end up arguing again.'

'You—came to—apologise . . .?' She couldn't believe it! *Rourke* apologise? 'What for?'

'For the way I acted this afternoon. I lacked understanding, and I was damned cruel to you.' He sighed. 'But I still think we'll be able to work something out.'

'I wish I could be as sure,' Clare said ruefully.

'How about we talk about it over dinner?'

'Dinner . . .?' she looked at him sharply.

'Yes.'

Her mouth twisted mockingly. 'What will Belinda have to say about that?' she taunted bitchily.

'Nothing,' he rasped.

'Nothing?'

'I told you, Clare,' he snapped, 'there's nothing between Belinda and me.'

Clare gave a deep sigh, tempted beyond endurance to have dinner with him. After all, why not? Harvey wouldn't be back in time, and she might already be too late to join Rena. Oh, why didn't she just admit, she *wanted* to have dinner with Rourke.

'I'd like to have dinner with you,' she accepted shyly.

His eyes widened. 'You would?'

She laughed, a slight catch to it. 'Changed your mind?'

'No,' he grinned. 'I'll meet you in ten minutes.'

'Make it fifteen,' she smiled, feeling suddenly light-hearted.

'You've got a deal. And, Clare,' he paused at the communicating door, 'I'll behave.'

'Behave . . .?'

He nodded. 'I won't try and force myself on you.'

Force! God, didn't he know by now that he didn't need to use *force*! She gave a bright smile. 'The minutes are ticking away,' she reminded him.

'Yes. Oh, and by the way, I've remembered something else Harvey said.'

'Yes?' she looked at him expectantly.

'He mentioned that he was at your mother's, so maybe he met someone there and went on to dinner.' Rourke went into his own suite, whistling softly to himself.

Her *mother's*! And Harvey had been delayed. She didn't like the sound of that, not at all. Lord, not Harvey too!

CHAPTER EIGHT

CLARE had a quick shower, feeling hot and sticky after her drive and time on the beach, and all the time she was dressing she was thinking of the implications of Harvey going to her mother's and somehow being delayed there.

Harvey was a handsome man, although not her mother's usual type, she would have thought. But then did her mother have a type? And as far as Carlene was concerned couldn't it be poetic justice?

That last fateful meeting with her mother had certainly opened Clare's eyes to her faults, so much so that she wouldn't be in the least surprised if she had made a play for Harvey. And she couldn't exactly blame him for being flattered by that attention, although she hoped he wouldn't get hurt. Her mother could be a bitch, and she wouldn't hesitate to get back at her for Rourke through Harvey, she knew that.

'Nearly ready?' Rourke strolled through from his own suite, buttoning his light blue shirt before tucking it into the low waistband of his navy blue trousers.

Clare's breath caught in her throat at the rugged virility of him, admiring the way the shirt and trousers fitted his masculinity, deepening the colour of his already deep blue eyes.

Those blue eyes widened now as they took in the clinging yellow dress she wore, revealing quite clearly that she wore little beneath it.

'You're playing with fire, you know that, don't you?' he said raggedly.

She finished brushing her hair about her shoulders, hoping he couldn't see the way her hand was shaking. 'I'm sorry?' She turned coolly to face him.

'That dress,' he muttered. 'I don't think you should wear it.'

'Really, Rourke,' she chided mockingly, 'I think I would cause more of a sensation if I didn't. Don't you?'

'Undoubtedly,' he ground out, his gaze never leaving her, fixed on her with burning intensity. 'But you must know, you can't have forgotten——'

No, she hadn't forgotten, but she would have thought he had. She had worn a dress very similar to this one the night they had made love, and it seemed Rourke remembered that too.

'This dress is a particular favourite of Harvey's,' she told him distantly, exaggerating somewhat. Harvey liked to see her in anything lemon or yellow, liked to perpetuate the image he had created for her, so she had no doubt he would have approved of the dress, but she could never remember him commenting on it one way or the other.

Rourke's mouth twisted. 'Don't worry, I'm not likely to forget you're engaged.'

After today Clare wasn't sure that was going to be true. If her mother really had got her claws into Harvey he might want to break off the engagement, and if he didn't then she just might. She could no more accept her mother's cast-offs now than she had five years ago.

'Neither am I.' She picked up her evening bag. 'I'm ready now.'

'I'm not,' Rourke scowled. 'Can you help me on with these?' and he held up a pair of cufflinks.

Her heart started hammering in her chest at the thought of going that close to him, of touching him. 'Of course,' she said coolly, moving forward with a confidence she was far from feeling. She took the gold cufflinks from him as he held out his wrists to her, hoping he wouldn't see how nervous she was, her hands shaking.

'Been practising?' he taunted as she did the first one up with no trouble, his warm breath fanning her cheek.

Clare kept her head bent, not managing the second clasp so easily, feeling all fingers and thumbs. 'I had to do it in one of my films.' She didn't rise to his baiting.

He was silent for several minutes as she continued to have trouble with the second cufflink. 'To an outsider,' he suddenly drawled, 'this could look quite a domesticated scene.'

'To an outsider, maybe,' she moved away as the second clasp clicked into place. 'To anyone who knows you, never,' she taunted.

Rourke quirked a mocking eyebrow. 'You don't see me as the pipe and slippers type?'

'Heavens, no!' she laughed.

A look of irritation flashed into his eyes, and then it was gone. 'Perhaps not,' he agreed tightly. 'I'll just get my jacket.'

They went to the Lady Hamilton Restaurant, as Rourke had an appetite for seafood, while Clare did not really care what she ate. Although once they were seated she found it a little uncomfortable to see Belinda Evans and about ten other cast members sitting just across the room from them, and as it was a long, not very wide room, it meant they were sitting very close indeed. In fact, they were greeted by several of them, jokes being made about 'the director and his leading lady', jokes that Rourke returned with lazy amusement.

'No fiancé tonight, Miss Anderson?' Only Belinda Evans could have asked such a thing!

Clare looked at the other girl with cold eyes, seeing the venom she didn't even try to hide. 'He's out on business,' she replied calmly.

'Really?' the other girl said with a wealth of meaning in her voice.

'Yes, really.' She raised a questioning eyebrow, as if daring Belinda to add to that.

She didn't, contenting herself with throwing resentful glances across the room at her.

'Little cat,' Rourke muttered.

Clare smiled. 'She likes you, that's all.'

'She's jealous, you mean?' His gaze was intense.

'I think so,' she nodded.

'And does she have reason to be?' he asked softly.

Her lids fluttered nervously, although she remained otherwise calm. 'I don't think so,' she answered quietly.

'Don't you?'

Her eyes were raised in alarm, looking away again as she saw the warmth in his gaze. 'Please, Rourke——'

'Yes?' he said huskily.

'We're here to talk business,' she reminded him determinedly.

'Yes,' he sighed, sitting back in his chair, surveying the room uninterestedly. 'Can we eat first?'

'Of course,' she nodded.

' "Of course",' he mimicked cruelly. 'What the hell happened to you in England?'

Anger blazed in her eyes. 'Nothing "happened" to me in England. If you remember, it happened before I went to England.'

'Hell, Clare, I'm sorry.' He sat forward to take her hand in his. 'I didn't mean to——'

'Let go of me!' She snatched her hand away and picked up her handbag. 'I don't think this was such a good idea. I'll eat in my room.'

'No!' The force behind the word kept her in her seat. 'I'm sorry,' he ran an agitated hand through the thickness of his hair, 'I said I would behave and I will.'

Clare sat stiffly in her seat. 'You aren't doing a very good job of it so far,' she said tightly.

'Clare, I——'

'Having trouble, darling?' drawled a seductive female voice.

Rourke didn't even look up. 'Get lost, Belinda,' he growled.

'I'm going, honey, I'm going.' She appeared unconcerned by his rudeness. 'The rest of us are going to get a drink in the Observation Bar, and I was elected to come over and ask you if you would like to join us later.'

'We may do,' he replied noncommittally.

Her hand came to rest on his shoulder. 'I'd like you to,' she said softly. 'If Miss Anderson is feeling tired, I'm sure she won't mind if you come alone,' she added hardly.

Rourke gave an angry sigh and shook off her hand. 'I said we may join you, Belinda,' he rapsed. 'And I meant "we". If Clare doesn't feel like going then neither will I.'

Blue eyes glittered angrily at Clare. As if it were all her fault! But Rourke was being exceptionally cruel to the girl. 'We would love to join you later, Belinda. Thank you,' she accepted softly.

If she had expected Belinda to be grateful for her intervention then she was out of luck. 'There you are, darling,' the other girl snapped at Rourke. 'You have your—Miss Anderson's permission. And if you're a good boy she may even let you drink alcohol!' She turned on her heel and whirled out of the room, her head held rebelliously high.

Clare looked tentatively at Rourke, sure that he was going to be furious about that last bitchy outburst. After all, Belinda had implied that she led him about by the nose! Instead of anger in Rourke's face she saw amusement, the deep blue eyes brimming with laughter.

'Rourke?' she queried in a surprised voice.

'Yes?' he smiled.

'You—you aren't angry?'

'No,' he shook his head.

'Really?'

'Really,' he confirmed, still smiling.

Clare began to smile herself now. 'It was rather funny, wasn't it?' she spluttered with laughter.

'It was,' he joined in the laughter. It was years since they had laughed together in this way, and Rourke obviously thought so too, his eyes showing his appreciation of her happiness. 'I always liked your laughter,' he told her softly.

'You liked to laugh *at* me,' she chided teasingly.

'Not nastily,' he contradicted.

No, it had never been in a cruel way, more like an indulgent lover. 'You weren't very nice to Belinda just now,' she said to hide her embarrassment.

'She deserved it,' he dismissed. 'I told you, I've only taken an interest in her because of her father. But much more of her baiting of you and I'll give her the good hiding she deserves.'

He meant it too. Poor Belinda!

The meal was delicious, all the more so because she and Rourke were friends again, were able to talk about every subject under the sun like they used to—with a few exceptions, of course, her mother being one of them, the end of their own relationship five years ago another.

They came to the end of their meal reluctantly, and lingered over their coffee. 'Do you want to join the others?' Rourke asked finally.

'I suppose we'd better,' she replied with some reluctance.

'We don't have to——'

'Oh, but we do, I told Belinda we would,' she teased.

'Damn Belinda,' he muttered. 'I don't want to be with you in a crowd, Clare.' His gaze was intent. 'I'm enjoying talking to you like this, being with you, alone.'

She was enjoying it too, which was why it had to end. She couldn't go through the heartache of five years ago all over again.

Rourke obviously saw her indecision. 'How about a walk round the deck?' he compromised. 'We can always join the others later. There's plenty of time.'

'I—It—Okay,' she decided. Why not? She was enjoying being with him too. And although she knew that might be dangerous she didn't yet have the willpower to bring the evening to a close. 'A walk would be nice,' she agreed.

'Good.' He pulled back her chair for her, his hand on her arm as they left the restaurant.

It was another beautiful evening, warm and clear, the stars shining brightly above them, the smog of the day seeming to have evaporated.

'So when do you intend getting married?' Rourke asked her suddenly.

'I don't know.' The question had taken her by surprise. 'When work commitments allow it, I suppose,' she added evasively.

'You aren't in any hurry, then?' he probed.

'Not really,' she shrugged. 'Harvey and I are quite happy as we are.' Rourke shook his head. 'That's where you're wrong.'

Clare looked at him sharply. Oh, lord, she hadn't given herself away, had she? Hadn't been enjoying his company so much she had let him guess she still loved him?

'Harvey isn't happy at all,' he added softly.

Harvey! He was talking about *Harvey*? 'I can assure you he is,' she spoke lightly in her relief.

Rourke shook his head. 'He didn't sound it the other evening.'

Colour tinged her cheeks. 'I can assure you that both of us are perfectly happy with our arrangement,' she said stiffly. Suddenly the evening had ceased to be enjoyable; Rourke's conversation was much too personal. She should have known she couldn't trust him, not even for one evening.

'How long have the two of you been engaged?'

'Just over a year. Rourke——'

'And neither of you wants to make it more permanent?' he probed relentlessly.

'It isn't a question——'

'You aren't right for each other, Clare——'

'And what would you know about it?' Her eyes flashed. 'What would *you* know about what's right for me?'

'I know what's wrong for you,' he told her grimly. 'And Harvey Pryce is wrong for you.'

'I don't happen to agree with you,' she snapped. 'Now, shall we join the others? I think we've—talked enough for one night.'

'Clare——'

She shook off his hand on her arm. 'Leave me alone! Haven't you done enough? Didn't you *do* enough?'

He seemed to go pale, his eyes deeply blue. 'I can't change the past——'

'And I won't let you change my future either,' she told him vehemently. 'I'm going to join the others, you please yourself whether or not you come along.'

'I'm coming,' he said grimly.

They walked in angry silence, arriving at the Observation Bar without having spoken a single word to each other. The other cast members welcomed them with some goodhearted teasing, although that soon stopped after Rourke scowled at them for several minutes.

'Come and sit beside me, darling,' Belinda invited him throatily.

'I thought you'd never ask,' he drawled.

Clare watched with pained eyes as he sat down beside the other girl, allowing her to snuggle up against him, the smile she shot in Clare's direction triumphant to say the least. Clare turned away, unable to watch the two of them together. Maybe she should go back to her room after all, maybe——

'Come and join us, Clare,' Rena interrupted her thoughts. 'Come and help me deal with these two flirting monsters,' she teased the two cameramen sitting either side of her.

Clare sat down, glad to have the decision to leave taken out of her hands, not wanting to go back to her room and brood, to be haunted by things that could never be. 'Giving you trouble, are they?' she grinned, ignoring Rourke and Belinda as the two of them whispered together.

Rena laughed. 'I keep telling them I'm married, but nothing seems to put them off.'

'Maybe they should meet Alan,' Clare teased. 'As I remember, he's an amateur boxing champion.'

'Ouch!' One of the men moved back with horror.

'Doesn't bother me,' the other one dismissed with a suggestive leer. 'I'm not bad at boxing myself.'

'Did I also mention that he's a judo black belt?' Rena asked innocently, joining in the game.

'Oh well, in that case . . .' Mark moved back too, turning pointedly to Clare. 'How about you? Are you available?'

' 'Fraid not,' and she laughingly flashed her engagement ring, telling herself she wasn't really aware of Belinda's throaty drawl or Rourke's lazy amusement.

Pete shook his head. 'Unless it's of the plain gold variety it doesn't count.' He moved nearer too.

'So much for fidelity?' Rena groaned in mock hurt.

This madness was exactly what Clare needed to help her ignore Rourke, and for the next hour she managed to do just that, laughing and joking with the other three.

But she was aware of Rourke's every movement, knew that he looked at her often—and that he was encouraging Belinda shamelessly. When the other couple stood up to leave she wasn't altogether surprised. She was determined not to go back to her own room yet, sure that tonight Rourke wasn't going to be alone. And she could no more listen to Rourke and Belinda together than she could stop loving Rourke herself.

Mark pulled a face. 'I suppose now that the boss has left we'll have to do the same.'

'I doubt Rourke intends going to sleep yet,' came her bitchy comment before she could stop herself.

'I doubt it too,' Pete chuckled. 'Still, it's one rule for him and another one for us. It's strange really, I worked with Rourke a few years ago, when he was just an actor, and he was a great guy to work with. I suppose your attitude has to change when you're the boss.'

'I suppose,' she agreed tightly.

'Come back to my room, Clare,' Rena invited. 'We can have some coffee and a chat.'

Clare looked at her friend, could see the compassion in her eyes. She had given herself away to Rena with that bitchy comment, although the two men seemed ignorant of her jealousy of Belinda Evans.

'Forget the coffee and the chat,' Mark grinned. 'And I'll come to your room.'

'I did say a black belt,' Rena reminded him.

'Spoilsport!' he grimaced.

Rena giggled. 'Come on, Clare, let's let these poor weary men get to bed.'

Rena kept up a constant stream of chatter as they walked to her room, ordering the coffee as soon as they got inside. 'Sit down, Clare.' She moved some magazines off a chair.

'If you would rather get to bed——'

'I wouldn't,' she insisted. 'Come on, I've ordered the coffee now,' she coaxed. 'Besides, I wanted to tell you this is going to be my last film, out of England anyway.'

'It is?' Clare's eyes widened as she sat down.

Rena shrugged. 'I told you it's getting harder and harder to leave Alan—well, he feels the same way. I was on the telephone half an hour last night trying to persuade him not to fly out here. He's so busy, he just doesn't have the time for mad escapades like that.'

'But I thought you loved acting,' Clare frowned.

'I did—I do. But I don't want to work for ever, and Alan seems to need me with him. I find that needing more thrilling than making any film,' her friend explained simply.

Clare felt a catch in her throat. Oh, how she wished she had someone who loved her like that, how she wished *Rourke* loved her like that.

Rena seemed to read something of her thoughts.

'Rourke isn't really interested in Belinda, you know,' she said gently.

'Rourke?' She feigned surprise, knowing she had never acted so badly in her life. 'Rourke's actions have nothing to do with me.'

'Don't they?'

'No!'

Rena sighed. 'That wasn't the impression I got tonight, from either of you.'

'Either of us . . .?'

Her friend shrugged. 'You had dinner together.'

'To discuss business,' Clare said tightly.

'Clare——'

'It's the truth, Rena.' She stood up in her agitation. 'You may have noticed that we don't work together very well?'

'Everyone has noticed that.'

'Well, we were trying to sort out our problems.'

Rena pulled a face. 'By the look of the two of you when you arrived in the bar it didn't work.'

'No,' Clare sighed, 'it didn't work.'

'Why?'

She looked up sharply. 'Why?' she repeated in a puzzled voice.

'Yes, why. I've worked with both of you in the past, and I know that ordinarily you're both very reasonable people. But together—well, together you're explosive. Everyone has noticed it, the catty Belinda with relish, I might add.'

Clare shrugged, knowing she couldn't tell anyone the real reason she didn't get on with Rourke. 'It's just a clash of personalities,' she dismissed. 'It happens.'

Rena still looked puzzled. 'It isn't like you, Clare. I've never known you not to get on with anyone.'

'There has to be the exception,' Clare said dryly.

'I don't—The coffee,' said Rena as a knock sounded on the door.

It was the necessary break in the conversation Clare

needed, and while they drank their coffee she managed to keep the other girl off the subject of Rourke and their antipathy for each other.

It was amazing what the two of them found to talk about once they got started, and it was after twelve when she finally made her way back to her own suite, sure that Rourke wouldn't still be entertaining Belinda next door.

The open communicating door showed that he hadn't brought Belinda back here at all. Thank goodness they had gone to Belinda's room. She closed the door.

'Clare!'

The door was being pushed open again, and she looked up into concerned blue eyes. 'Rourke!' she breathed huskily. He seemed to have come out of the bathroom, for he was wearing only a towelling robe and his hair was slightly damp from the shower he had taken.

'God, Clare!' he groaned in a tortured voice. 'I thought you'd gone off with one of those clowns.'

'I've been talking to Rena——'

'Not Mark or Pete?'

'Certainly not!'

'Thank God for that, I would have ripped him apart—God, Clare, why do we have to keep hurting each other?' He reached out for her.

Thoughts of him and Belinda made her cringe back. 'No!'

'Clare, I want you!' he moaned.

'No!' she shuddered now. 'Where's Belinda?'

'How the hell should I know?' His eyes hardened.

'You left with her——'

'And you know why! We're destroying each other, Clare. Bit by bit we're slowly destroying each other. And all because we really want each other.'

'I don't want you!' she denied heatedly. 'Now, would you mind leaving? I have to call Harvey.'

'Harvey!' he snapped in an icy voice. 'Finish with him and we can——'

'*We* can't do anything. I wouldn't do anything with you even if I weren't engaged to Harvey. What happened that night five years ago destroyed any feeling I might ever have had for you,' she lied, protecting herself in any way she could.

Rourke drew in a ragged breath. 'Then I guess there's nothing left to say.'

'Nothing at all,' she agreed tightly.

'I won't bother you again.'

'I hope you don't.'

'If only you——'

'Goodnight, Rourke,' Clare said pointedly.

He didn't answer, turning on his heel and going back into his own suite, the door locking behind him.

Clare sank shakily into a chair. It was over, finally over. Rourke wouldn't go back on his word, she had seen that in his eyes.

He had been offering her another affair. God, she thought, hadn't he done her enough damage the first time around! He finally seemed to have got the message, although what it would do for an already strained working relationship she had no idea.

And right now she refused to even think about it. She had told Rourke she was going to call Harvey, and that was what she did, longing for the reassuring sound of his voice.

There was no answer from his room. She tried again, still no answer. Harvey wasn't even back yet! The second time she had deliberately let the telephone ring, knowing that if Harvey were there but asleep he would have answered it. He hadn't come back!

Oh God, her mother had done it again! How could she, how *dared* she? And Harvey had let her down in the worst way possible.

She thought of telephoning her mother's house to confirm her suspicions, but her pride wouldn't allow for that. Besides, at this time of night it was obvious what they would be doing. And she refused to speak to Harvey when he was in her mother's bed!

She was aware of her lack of trust in Harvey, and yet it wasn't really that, it was her knowledge of her mother's true nature that made her believe what she did. No one could blame Harvey, if her mother had made a play for him he wouldn't be able to refuse. She had seen her mother in action, and no man was immune to her—not even Rourke!

Strange, she was still more hurt by Rourke's past betrayal than she was by Harvey's present-day one. Perhaps not so strange—she still loved him, damn him!

She spent a restless night, finally getting up and dressing when it became obvious she wasn't going to get any sleep. As soon as it was a reasonable time she tried Harvey's room again, but there was still no answer. She hadn't expected anything else, not really. Although what they would say to each other when he did return she had no idea.

Just as she was about to leave her room the telephone rang. She snatched up the receiver, at the same time wondering whether she should have been worried about Harvey instead of mentally berating him. What if he had been involved in an accident, what if this were the police or hospital calling to let her know——

It wasn't, it was the reception desk. 'Mr Pryce came back late last night,' the girl informed her. 'But he left again more or less straight away. He left a message for you.'

'Yes?' Clare instantly tensed.

'We did try to reach you, but there was no answer in your room, and we had no idea where we could get in touch with you. Mr Pryce left instructions we weren't to disturb you until this morning.'

'Yes?' Clare prompted again.

'He wanted you to know that he was well, and that he would telephone you later today.'

'Is that all?' she asked in a disappointed voice.

'Yes, Miss Anderson.' The girl sounded as puzzled as she was.

'Thank you,' and Clare rang off, staring sightlessly into space.

Harvey was all right and he would call her later today! What was that supposed to mean?

She hurried from her room, determined not to be late. There had been no morning cup of coffee brought to her by Rourke today, but luckily she had been up early enough to order some for herself. Somehow she had missed Rourke bringing in her morning cup of coffee, and the little chat they usually had. It had usually been stimulating if nothing else!

By the time of her first scene of the day she was calm and composed, Harvey's enigmatic message pushed to the back of her mind. She never wore her engagement ring during filming, and somehow today she didn't think she would ever be wearing it again.

It wasn't all Harvey's fault, he was engaged to a woman who loved another man, and maybe he had been sensitive to that. Even if he hadn't gone off with her mother she would have had to call off their engagement. Harvey deserved all a woman's love, not a portion of it.

'Ready, Miss Anderson?'

'Yes,' she answered Rourke huskily. She had been 'Miss Anderson' all morning, showing her that there really was 'nothing more to say'. His chilling politeness made it easier for her to work with him, although only as a director; their scenes together were still cancelled.

Working for him was better than working with him, and by the end of the day she was quite satisfied with her performance. Rourke seemed to be too, none of the biting criticism she was used to being forthcoming today.

Harvey still hadn't telephoned as she changed back into her own clothes and handed her costume to Wendy, the wardrobe girl. And as he hadn't called she had no idea what she was going to do about Gene coming to dinner this evening. Harvey could be back in time, but even if he were she wasn't sure she wanted to have dinner with him, let alone have him meet Gene.

She had tried telephoning Gene at lunchtime to put him off for tonight, but the old telephone number she had for him was out of service, evidence that he had moved. She had no other way of getting in touch with him, so Harvey or no Harvey, she was having dinner with Gene tonight.

She didn't feel like having dinner with anyone; she felt suddenly lost and alone without Harvey's emotional support. During the past three years she had come to rely on his professional and emotional support, and without him she felt somehow defenceless.

'No fiancé again, Miss Anderson?'

She almost groaned aloud at the sound of that taunting female voice. 'Harvey is never here when we're working,' she answered Belinda calmly enough, although by the light of battle in the other girl's eyes this conversation was far from over.

Belinda sauntered over with exaggerated grace, her denims skin-tight, and obviously wearing no bra beneath the silky blouse. 'The way I heard it,' she drawled, 'he's gone.'

'Then you heard it wrong.' Clare's voice was brittle.

'Did I?' the other girl persisted.

'Yes,' she snapped. 'I don't know where you got your information——'

'The front desk,' Belinda taunted.

Clare swallowed hard, determined not to show any emotion in front of this girl. 'Then they're mistaken,' she said tightly. 'Harvey has gone away on business for a couple of days, but he'll be back.'

'Will he?'

'Yes!'

'You're sure he didn't take exception to the way you drool over Rourke and broke off your engagement?' Belinda scorned.

It was so far from the truth that she had to smile. 'I'm very sure about that.'

The other girl flushed with anger. 'You're making a fool of yourself, you know.'

Clare eyed her pityingly. 'I don't think I'm the one doing that.'

Belinda's eyes glittered vehemently. 'Don't get clever with me,' she snapped. 'You don't mean a thing to Rourke. You just represent a challenge to him, and once you've given him what he wants he won't be interested any more.'

This was nearer the truth—as Clare knew from experience. 'The same applies to you, Belinda,' she said coolly. 'I should remember that.'

'Snobby bitch!' the other girl muttered before marching off.

'Wow!' Wendy came out from behind some clothes, her eyes wide. 'That's one jealous young lady!'

Clare laughed. 'Don't worry about it, I'm not going to.'

And she didn't. Belinda was so obviously suffering from unrequited interest that it wasn't worth thinking about. Rourke was playing with the girl's affections, but then that was none of her business, Belinda was old enough to take care of herself. More than old enough!

What was her affair was the claim she had made that Harvey had left the ship completely. *That* was her business, and Clare went straight to the reception desk to confirm or deny the claim.

She couldn't believe it—but it was true! The girl on the desk told her that Harvey had booked out yesterday evening when he left the message for her. She wasn't sure of the time, only that he was no longer staying on the *Queen Mary*.

Clare wasn't even aware of returning to her suite, she was too dazed to know what she was doing. Surely Harvey hadn't moved in with her mother on the basis of such a short acquaintance? It was an impetuous act, and it didn't sound like Harvey at all. None of this sounded like him, not the disappearing act, or his silence since.

Once again she was tempted to telephone her mother, but once again she decided against it. She simply couldn't talk to that women, couldn't——

'Clare?' A knock sounded on the outside door, and Rourke's voice was unmistakable. 'Clare, can I talk to you?'

She didn't feel up to talking to anyone right now, she was too stunned by Harvey's defection. 'Could it wait until later?'

'I'd rather it was now.'

She sighed, and moved to open the door before sitting down again, too numb to care what Rourke thought of her behaviour.

'The little bitch!' he muttered, coming to stand in front of her. 'I'm sorry, Clare. I wouldn't have had you subjected to that for anything. When I get hold of her——'

She gave an irritated frown. 'What are you talking about, Rourke?'

'Belinda,' he growled. 'Wendy told me how she spoke to you. I can see how it's upset you.' He frowned down at her.

'No, you can't, Rourke.' Clare gave a brittle laugh. 'The things your little girl-friend said meant nothing to me. Less than nothing.'

'Then what——'

The telephone began ringing, and Clare snatched up the receiver before it could ring a second time. 'Harvey!' she sighed her relief as she recognised his voice. 'Harvey, where are you?'

'So that's it,' Rourke rasped. 'I'm sorry I bothered you.' He moved to the door.

'Rourke——' Too late, he had gone, closing the door forcefully behind him. 'No, Harvey, of course you haven't interrupted anything,' she said sharply. 'Now where are you? The receptionist told me you've booked out.'

'I have. Oh, Clare, I don't know where to start, what to say,' he groaned.

She could hear the anguish in his voice. 'Just tell me, Harvey,' she encouraged softly.

'I—I'm in Las Vegas——'

'Las Vegas?' she echoed shrilly.

'Yes. I—I got married this afternoon, Clare.'

Married! She couldn't believe it. Harvey had married her mother!

CHAPTER NINE

'CLARE?' Harvey's anxiety came clearly down the telephone line. 'Darling, are you all right?'

'I—Yes,' she swallowed hard. 'You—you're married?'

'Yes,' he sighed. 'I never wanted to hurt you, Clare. I just couldn't help myself.'

'I understand,' she said dully, knowing she didn't understand at all. Harvey *married* to her mother!

'I just couldn't help it,' he repeated softly, almost to himself. 'As soon as I saw her—I just didn't know what had hit me!'

'No.'

'Clare . . .? God, Clare, I wish I didn't have to hurt you like this.'

'It's all right, Harvey. Really it is.' Harvey was her *stepfather*! Not Rourke at all, but *Harvey*. She didn't know whether to laugh or cry.

'As soon as I saw her again——'

'Again?' she echoed sharply. Surely Harvey had never met her mother before?

'I haven't explained myself very well,' he said ruefully. 'I'm just so—well, I'm not exactly myself.'

She could tell that, could hear the ecstatic happiness in his voice. 'Maybe you should explain, Harvey.' After all, he owed her that much.

'Well, I went to your mother's yesterday afternoon——'

'Yes, I know that.'

'Somerville told you?'

Clare blushed. 'Yes. Harvey, about Rourke being in my room, that didn't have anything to do with this—hasty marriage, did it?'

'No,' he laughed. 'In fact, I'm not even going to ask *what* he was doing in your room.'

'He——'

'You don't owe me any explanations, Clare,' he cut in gently. 'I knew from the first that there was something between you, and your mother told me——'

'She told you?' Clare cut in angrily. 'She had no right to do that! It was years ago.'

'But you still love him,' Harvey said gently. 'And your mother telling me Rourke was the man from the past helped me feel less guilty about letting you down the way I have.'

Trust her mother, she never missed a trick! 'Carry on, Harvey,' Clare sighed.

'Well, your mother had a pool-party going on.'

'She always does,' Clare said dryly.

'Mm, only this one was different. As soon as I saw Shara again I——'

'Shara?' she repeated sharply. 'Your Shara?'

He laughed huskily. 'Well, she is now, but she wasn't then.'

'You're married to Shara Morgan?'

'Yes,' he confirmed in a puzzled voice. 'Who else would I be married to so suddenly?'

Who else indeed? Her imagination had been working overtime. Her imagination and her past knowledge of her mother.

She gave a relieved laugh. 'Congratulations, Harvey.'

'You really mean that?'

'I really do,' she said sincerely. 'You must be very happy.'

'I am. I feel guilty about you, but——'

'You have no need to feel that way. My mother was right,' she lowered her voice in case Rourke should be in his suite, not wanting him to overhear the conversation, 'I did know Rourke in the past.'

'And you might get back together now?' he asked hopefully.

'We might,' she evaded, not wanting to mar Harvey's happiness on his wedding day. She might have lost him, but he had Shara back, and she could tell how happy that made him. 'Tell me about you and Shara,' she encouraged.

He was only too happy to talk about his brand-new wife. As soon as he and Shara had seen each other again they had known they had made a mistake splitting up four years ago. Shara realised that her career wasn't enough, that she wanted Harvey too.

'I couldn't believe it, Clare,' he added excitedly. 'It was as if the last four years had never happened, as if we'd never been apart.'

'I know, Harvey, I know,' she said sadly.

'God, I must sound so damned selfish to you,' he misunderstood the reason for her sadness. 'Our friendship meant a lot to me, Clare. I don't want you to think it didn't.'

Friendship? Yes, that was truly all it was, with perhaps a little sexual attraction on Harvey's side, but even that hadn't been as strong on her part. 'It meant a lot to me too, Harvey,' she told him warmly. 'You helped restore my faith in men, and believe me, it had taken a heavy knock.'

'Somerville again?'

'Yes.'

'But everything is all right between you now?'

'Yes,' she agreed to put his mind at rest. 'Does this mean I've lost my manager?' she teased.

'Oh lord, I hadn't given that a thought——'

'Of course you haven't,' she chuckled. 'And I don't expect you to. I'm thinking of taking a holiday after this film, anyway, so there won't be anything to manage for a while. Now, you'd better get back to your bride. And give Shara my congratulations.'

'Thank you, Clare,' he said softly. 'You really have been very understanding.'

'Just be happy,' she told him with a catch in her voice.

'Maybe I can be godmother to your first child?'

'It's a deal,' he said excitedly, the idea of a child obviously just occurring to him. 'Take care, Clare.'

'You too.'

'And I'll see you soon.'

'Harvey, will you get off the phone!' she laughed. 'Before Shara gets fed up waiting for you!'

She was still smiling as she put the telephone down. Lucky Harvey! At least things had worked out well for him.

But now what was she going to do? Harvey had been her defence, her refuge that she could always hide behind when Rourke threatened to get too close. Now she was going to have to fight him on her own.

Her engagement ring was locked away in her jewellery box from this morning, and she left it there. She would return it to Harvey when she saw him next.

Right now she was going to have to have dinner with Gene alone, all the time pretending that Harvey was still her loving fiancé. Perhaps she wouldn't see Rourke. Too much probing from him and she was likely to lose her temper and tell him everything.

But maybe he wouldn't even speak to her——the way he had slammed out of here when Harvey telephoned seemed to indicate that would be the case. Anyway, Gene would be with her, and he knew she wasn't likely to want to be alone with Rourke.

She was in the bath when the knock sounded on the door, and water was still streaming off her as she hastily pulled on a robe before answering it. 'Gene!' she frowned her consternation as he beamed at her. 'But it's only just gone six o'clock!'

'I know,' he nodded happily, stepping inside, carrying a jacket and shirt on a hanger. 'I checked with the desk here and found out the tour lasts about two hours, and it closed at five-thirty, so I had to get here early this afternoon. I took a walk around the deck to waste a bit more time, and—well, here I am.'

She closed the door. 'Yes, here you are. And what's that?' she indicated the clothes on the hanger.

He grinned, laying the things down in a chair. 'Well, I can hardly take Clare Anderson out to dinner dressed like this,' he looked down pointedly at the bright yellow tee-shirt he wore, 'I LIKE IT' emblazoned across the front of it.

Clare didn't need two guesses what 'IT' was, and a reluctant smile lightened her features. 'No, I suppose not. Would you like to use the shower?'

'I thought you'd never ask.'

She shook her head. 'You never change. Give me ten minutes to dry myself—properly, and dress, and then the bathroom is all yours.'

'Thanks.' He settled himself into one of the armchairs. 'Nice suite,' he looked round appreciatively. 'Did you know that over fifty-six different sorts of wood——'

'Not you too!' she laughed. 'I heard all this from Harvey.'

'No sense of history some people,' he muttered jokingly.

'I won't be long,' she smiled.

It took her slightly longer than ten minutes to get herself ready, but Gene's appreciative comments about the black dress she wore showed he wasn't annoyed by the wait.

'See you soon.' He took his fresh clothing into the bathroom with him, closing the door.

In his absence Clare applied her make-up, light lipgloss and mascara—the dress was dramatic enough. It had thin shoulder-straps, dipping very low over her breasts, showing a large expanse of creamy flesh, the clinging material clearly showing the taut nipples beneath, the rest of the gown loose-fitting down to its knee-length, hinting at the provocative curves beneath, the chiffon of the material giving a ghostly outline of her body.

It was a dress that made her feel totally feminine,

gave her confidence, and for the rest of the making of this film she was going to need plenty of that.

When a second knock sounded on the door her heart stopped beating. Rourke had a distinctive way of knocking on the door, when he bothered to do so, and she knew that this was him.

'Yes?' she greeted him coolly.

His gaze ran over her slowly, his eyes a deeper blue by the time they reached her face. 'Beautiful,' he said throatily.

She stiffened. 'Did you want something, Rourke?'

'That's like asking a thirsty man in a desert if he would like a drink of water,' he said sardonically.

Her cheeks suffused with colour. 'Would you please just tell me why you're here and then leave,' she told him stiltedly.

'Belinda told me——'

'Hey, Clare, this robe of yours is——' Gene broke off, his expression a comical mixture of consternation and amusement.

Clare felt like laughing herself, hysterically. This was like something out of a farce, all the characters frozen into immobility. Gene had come out of the bedroom towelling his hair dry, wearing only her robe, which was obviously much too small for his muscular frame, only just decent.

And it was obvious from Rourke's thunderous expression what construction he had put on the situation. His expression was contemptuous, his eyes like chips of ice as he looked at the two of them.

Gene was the first to break the stunned silence. 'Rourke,' he greeted politely.

'Lester,' Rourke rasped. 'I had no idea Clare was seeing you again.'

'Oh, but I——'

'I never could stay away from Clare,' Gene cut in cheerfully, obviously recovered from his surprise at seeing Rourke here and now about to enjoy the situation.

'Not many men can,' Rourke replied tautly.

'No,' Gene agreed laughingly.

'Especially her fiancé,' Rourke added pointedly.

Gene moved forward to put his arm about Clare's shoulders, the robe going even higher up his thighs. 'I'm a friend of Clare's.' He looked challengingly at Rourke.

'Aren't we all!' Rourke snapped before turning on his heel and leaving.

'Whew!' Gene raised his eyebrows. 'I have this feeling I should be lying dead right now!'

Clare's eyes sparkled angrily. 'If you aren't you should be,' she agreed angrily. 'You deliberately let him think——'

'What he was already thinking,' Gene finished softly. 'Boy, talk about jealous!'

'Don't be ridiculous!' she snapped. 'He was probably disgusted. I am engaged, you know.'

'Rourke couldn't give a damn about your fiancé,' he scorned. 'He was jealous on his own behalf.'

'Rubbish——'

'Hey, this is Gene, remember?' he said softly. 'And that guy was so jealous he would have liked to hit me.'

'Then why did you bait him like that?' she demanded.

He shrugged. 'Maybe I thought he deserved it.'

'Oh, Gene!' she shook her head. 'You——'

'That man has the power to hurt you,' he insisted. 'And I won't let him. I've only just got you back,' he added lightly, 'and I'm not going to risk you disappearing again for another five years.'

Clare gave a reluctant laugh. 'Go and get dressed, you look ridiculous.'

He pulled a face. 'That's what I was about to tell you when I came in here and got stabbed with a pair of icy blue eyes. God, I'd hate to meet him in a dark alley when I'm on my own!' He went off muttering to himself.

Clare's smile instantly faded. Gene had unwittingly

stumbled across Rourke's true nature. He was a street-
fighter first and foremost. Beneath the veneer of con-
ventionality he displayed to the world was the man who
had been abandoned as a child, the man who as a boy
had been cruelly rejected by his mother, the man who
had been determined to get to the top even if he had to
claw his way up there.

He wasn't a man she should ever have become
involved with, in her maturity she could see that, but
even knowing that, she still loved him, would always love
him. And that was why tonight she had to be more self-
possessed than usual. As far as she knew no one else
was aware of the fact that she was no longer engaged, but
even so, when the news did break she didn't intend looking
an idiot.

'Very nice,' she told Gene when he came back in the
clean shirt and jacket. 'I'll probably have a hard job
keeping the women off you,' she teased, her arm through
his as they made their way to the restaurant.

'I hope so,' he grinned down at her. 'Shouldn't we be
calling for your fiancé?'

She blushed, unable to meet his gaze. 'Harvey is
away—on business,' she evaded. 'So he won't be joining
us.'

'Pity. Hey, I hear music.'

'Yes,' she said with some relief, glad that he had
accepted her explanation for Harvey's absence so easily.
'They dance on deck Friday and Saturday evenings, to
the ship's band.'

'And today being Friday . . .'

'Exactly,' she nodded.

'Dancing under the stars,' he murmured. 'I always knew I
was a romantic at heart.'

'*You* are?' Clare spluttered with laughter.

'Yes, me,' he pretended insult, opening the restaurant
door for her. 'See?'

'Opening the door for a woman doesn't make you a
romantic,' she giggled.

Gene confirmed that they had a table booked. 'Like a drink first?' he suggested.

'Lovely,' she nodded.

The meal in the Sir Winston, as last time, was superb. And as each course progressed and there was no sign of Rourke or Belinda to mar her evening Clare felt herself relaxing and enjoying herself, drinking more wine than usual as Gene entertained her with the more amusing Hollywood gossip.

She had just finished laughing at one of the more uproarious tales when Rourke and Belinda walked in. Her humour instantly faded, and she turned to look out of the window, ignoring them.

'Who is *that*?' Gene asked in a whisper.

'Rourke——'

'Not him, woman,' he growled. 'The little beauty with him.'

'Belinda.' She pulled a face.

'Of course, Belinda Evans,' he nodded recognition. 'But you don't share my appreciation?'

Clare shrugged moodily. The evening was ruined now. Why couldn't the other couple have eaten in the Capstan or the Lady Hamilton, why *here*?

'Does that mean you don't?' Gene prompted.

'It means I'm uninterested.'

'I would say you were the opposite,' he chuckled. 'A little jealous yourself, Clare?'

'Like hell I am,' she snapped. 'I don't give a damn.'

'Now I know you're jealous,' he taunted. 'You never used to swear, Clare.'

'I've changed——'

'Not that much. You never liked anyone who swore, I remember that very well.'

'I've got used to it,' she shrugged.

'Not so much that you would swear yourself—unless you were provoked. Miss Evans rubs you up the wrong way, hmm?'

'Believe me,' she said bleakly, 'the dislike is mutual.'

'I can see why—you're both fighting over the same man.'

'We are not——'

'Liar!' Gene admonished softly. 'I'd be prepared to take the lovely Belinda out of the picture if you'd like me to.'

'Why on earth should I want that?' she flashed. 'I'm engaged——'

'No, you aren't,' Gene contradicted gently.

Clare gave him a startled look. 'I—I'm not?'

'No,' he shook his head. 'Shara is a big star in this country, her marriage is going to hit the front page of the newspapers.'

Clare picked up her glass of wine with a shaking hand, taking a deep swallow, almost choking over it. 'You—you knew all the time?'

He nodded. ' 'Fraid so.'

She licked her lips. 'How?'

'Shara works for Dad's studio. He was furious about the fact that she'd just gone off without telling him. It was all he could talk about at lunch. And he wanted to know who the hell Harvey Pryce is,' he added dryly.

'Poor Harvey!' Clare's mouth twisted.

'Oh, don't worry, after finding out the facts Dad's building it up into a really big romantic story—you know, childhood sweethearts and all that.'

'Hardly childhood,' Clare derided.

Gene grinned. 'By the time Dad's finished they'll have known each other from the cradle!'

'And I'm going to come out of it looking like a fool,' she sighed, her worst fears realised.

'Not now, you have me. After all, I'm not a bad replacement,' and he gave her a hopeful look.

She couldn't help smiling. 'Not bad at all. And I really do want Harvey to be happy with Shara, you know.'

'Yes, I do know. You don't have it in you to begrudge them their happiness.'

She pulled a face. 'I'm not a paragon, Gene. And I

am going to look pretty stupid once the news breaks.'

'To Rourke, you mean?'

'No, I don't mean!' she snapped. 'I couldn't care less about——'

'Liar,' he said again. 'They're sitting in the other room, by the way.'

She swallowed her relief. 'They are?'

'Mm. I can't even see them.'

Clare visibly relaxed. 'Are you ready to dance with me under the stars?' she attempted lightness.

'As long as you promise not to seduce me.'

She once again spluttered with laughter. 'You're impossible!' she chuckled as they left the restaurant.

'But I make you laugh.'

'Yes,' she smiled. 'And I'm grateful for that.'

The dancing at the back of the ship was well under way by the time they joined the other couples on the Promenade Deck, with the *Queen Mary* orchestra playing above them.

'This really is romantic.' Gene nuzzled into her hair.

'Don't get carried away,' Clare warned.

'Allow a man his dreams,' he murmured.

Gene's lighthearted flirting was exactly what she needed to bolster her ego, and she was glowing by the time she saw Rourke and Belinda standing on the edge of the crowd watching the people dancing.

She instantly felt selfconscious. 'I think I've had enough for now, Gene,' she muttered.

'Mm?' Gene raised his head to look down at her.

'Let's rest a while, hmm?'

'Okay,' he shrugged. 'I——'

'Can I cut in?' drawled a familiar voice.

Clare stiffened, turning to face Rourke. 'We were just going to sit down.'

'I only want one dance, Clare.' His eyes were icy.

Her mouth twisted. 'Won't Belinda mind?' She looked pointedly at the glowering girl standing where he had left her.

'No, she won't mind.' Surprisingly it was Gene who answered her. 'Because I'll go and keep her company.'

Rourke's eyes narrowed. 'You will?'

'Sure,' the other man nodded. 'I've been longing to meet her. See you later, Clare.'

She glared after him, as she moved mechanically into Rourke's arms. She could kill Gene later.

'Not very flattering,' Rourke drawled.

She was very conscious of being close to him, of the sensuously male aura that never failed to weaken her resolve not to be affected by him. And he was wearing a tangy, elusive aftershave, his hands warm and possessive as they rested on her hips.

'Gene is perfectly free to dance with whom he chooses to,' she said stiltedly.

Rourke's hands tightened painfully. 'As you're free to go to bed with whom you want?' he rasped.

'*If* I want, yes,' she nodded coolly, surprised at her confidence. It was as she had thought, Rourke believed she and Gene had been to bed together earlier this evening.

'And you did want, didn't you!' His fingers dug into her flesh. 'Hell, Clare, why not me?' he groaned. 'If you had to go to bed with some man to get back at Pryce——'

'Get back at him?' she echoed sharply.

'For going off and leaving you,' he dismissed tersely. 'Belinda told me he's gone——'

'Only on business!'

'Oh yes?'

'Yes!'

Rourke closed his eyes momentarily, those same eyes blazing into hers as he lifted his lids. 'I couldn't give a damn whether he's gone for good or just a few days. If you *had* to sleep with someone why couldn't you have chosen me? Why, Clare?'

She licked her lips nervously. 'Because I don't want to go to bed with you——'

'You do, damn you!' he rasped. 'I can't believe your reactions to me don't mean something.'

'It means it's easier to give in to you than fight. Fighting never got me anywhere last time,' she added bitterly.

Rourke's hands instantly dropped to his sides. 'Why must you always remind me of that?'

'Because I can't forget it!'

His mouth was a thin, angry line. 'I'll take you back to Lester.'

She wasn't sure Gene wanted her back. He was laughing and joking with Belinda as they approached them, the other girl basking in his flirtateous attention. Gene shot Clare a wink as he turned, his arm going about her shoulders.

'Back so soon?' he asked mischievously.

Her fingernails dug into his side where her own arm was about his waist. 'Mr Somerville realised I was—tired.'

'Would you like to dance, Belinda?' Rourke held out his hand to the other girl.

Belinda didn't even hesitate, moulding herself to him as they moved slowly together to the music.

'Could we leave, Gene?' Clare asked him raggedly.

'Sure,' he agreed easily. 'Let's go for a walk.'

She would rather have gone to her room, but she fell into step beside him. After all, he was her guest for the evening, it was hardly polite to run to her room and hide just because Rourke had once again unnerved her.

'Does Rourke know about Harvey yet?'

The question was to be expected. 'He knows he's gone, he doesn't know why,' she answered dully.

'Clare, is Harvey a shield to you?'

She frowned. 'A shield?'

He nodded. 'Against Rourke.'

'Hardly,' she scorned. 'Believe me, my engagement hasn't stopped Rourke doing exactly what he wants to do.'

'And that is?'

'Kissing me whenever he's in the mood!' Clare admitted angrily.

'And is he "in the mood" often?' Gene quirked a questioning eyebrow.

'He—I——' she licked her lips nervously. 'Quite often,' she mumbled.

'Mm, that's what I thought. Little Miss Sex-bomb is jealous of you, you know.'

'She has no reason——'

'Doesn't she?' he shook his head. 'I've watched the two of you together, and I think she has good reason.'

'No——'

'Yes. Rourke can't take his eyes off you. But then he never could,' he added ruefully. 'From the first day you met you sent sparks off each other.'

'Sexual attraction!' Clare snapped.

'For whom?'

'For both of us!'

'Like hell,' Gene smiled. 'You didn't even know what sexual attraction was. And Rourke looked as if someone had hit him.'

'Rubbish!'

'It's the truth,' he insisted. 'Clare, do you have any idea why Rourke is here?'

She gave an impatient sigh. 'To direct the film,' she said as if talking to a two-year-old.

He nodded. 'But why?'

'Jason Faulkner had an accident——'

'And Rourke was due to start work on another movie.'

'Which he couldn't do because of the revolution.'

Gene frowned. 'What revolution?'

'Oh, don't be dense, Gene,' she snapped irritably. 'You were due to work on the film too, you must know the reason it was cancelled.'

'Yes, I do,' he nodded.

'Well, then . . .'

'And it wasn't because of any revolution,' he dismissed. 'We were all put on hold because Rourke chose to direct this movie instead of *Gun Serenade*.'

Clare gaped at him. 'I don't understand. Rourke told me—He said——'

'Yes?'

'You mean he really wanted to do this film?' she gasped, very pale. 'Chose to do it instead of *Gun Serenade*?'

'Obviously,' Gene drawled.

'But why?' she voiced the same question Gene had seconds earlier.

He shrugged. 'I would have thought that was obvious too.'

'Not to me,' she shook her head.

'Because of you, Clare,' he said patiently. 'Because it gave Rourke the opportunity to see you again.'

'No ...'

'Yes.'

Could she believe that? *Dared* she believe it?

CHAPTER TEN

OF course Gene had to be wrong. There was no reason
to suppose Rourke had any desire to see her again. If he
had felt anything like she did about the meeting then he
hadn't wanted it at all, had only discovered he still felt
sexual attraction towards her after being forced to meet
her again.

'Stop torturing yourself, Clare,' Gene frowned as the
different emotions flitted across her face. 'You know
damn well it's the truth.'

'Of course I don't! I never heard anything so ridiculous!'

'And I never *saw* anything as ridiculous as the two of
you trying to look as if you didn't give a damn about
the other. Let's sit down,' Gene dragged her over to a
bench placed on the deck. 'Now tell me the real reason
the two of you broke up five years ago. And I mean the
real reason,' he warned.

Clare stared straight ahead of her. 'We weren't
suited——'

'In or out of bed?'

'Out of—Gene!' she gave him an angry glare. 'That
was unfair!'

He gave a rueful smile. 'So it was out of bed. But you
loved him, Clare——'

'And he loved my mother!' There, it was said, the
dark painful secret that she had buried in her subcon-
scious until it had ceased to cause that raw pain that she
hadn't been able to forget the first two years of being in
London.

Gene frowned his puzzlement. 'What are you talking
about? *Rourke* loved Carlene?'

'You know he did,' she flashed angrily. 'Everyone

174

knew of their affair—except me.'

'Affair? But there was no affair.'

'But you said yourself——'

'That your mother was interested in Rourke,' he nodded. 'But he certainly wasn't interested in her.'

'He was——'

'Never,' Gene insisted emphatically.

Clare swallowed hard, looking down at her hands. 'You're wrong. You see, I—I saw them—in bed together,' she revealed shakily.

Gene's frown deepened. 'I can't believe that,' he shook his head.

'Why not? Didn't you warn me not to get involved with him?'

'Yes, but not for that reason.' He stood up to begin pacing the deck. 'God, not because of Rourke and your mother! Rourke was never interested in her——'

'He was in her bed!' Clare interrupted heatedly.

'I couldn't give a damn about what you saw, or what you *think* you saw——'

'Oh, I saw it all right,' she recalled bitterly.

'Whatever you saw Rourke had not been making love to your mother,' Gene said firmly. 'He despised her, he always has.'

All colour left Clare's face. 'I can't believe that.'

'Believe me, it's true. My father directed them both six years ago, and Rourke nearly walked out half a dozen times.'

'*Rourke* did?' It didn't sound like him at all.

'Yes,' Gene nodded. 'Your mother was impossible.'

'She has a temper,' Clare agreed.

'Not because of her temper, Clare. She wanted Rourke, and she was determined to get him in any way she could. But Rourke didn't want to know.'

'Just an act,' she shrugged dismissively. 'To make my mother more interested.'

'So much of an act that Rourke threatened to leave if Dad didn't get her off his back?'

She swallowed hard. 'He did?'

'He sure did. Dad was pulling his hair out until the end of the movie. But even then your mother didn't give up, inviting Rourke over to the house every opportunity she could. Rourke had to give in occasionally, otherwise the press might have picked up on his antagonism, but he made sure he was never alone with your mother, that they always met in a crowd.'

'Then that afternoon I met him . . .?'

'Only the third time he'd ever been there. And even then he kept himself distant from the rest of us.'

Clare remembered seeing Rourke in the pool while everyone else lounged about it, had thought even then that he didn't quite fit in with her mother's usual crowd. 'Then what was he doing in my mother's bed?' she asked slowly.

'I have no idea.' Gene put his hands in his trousers pockets. 'But I do know he wasn't making love to her.' He shrugged. 'Your mother is a very devious woman, Clare, in fact that was the reason I warned you about seeing Rourke. Your mother will stop at nothing to get what she wants.'

Nothing . . .? Her heart gave a sickening lurch. *Could* she have misjudged that situation five years ago? Impossible! Rourke had been in her mother's bed, her mother in her négligé, there could be no other explanation other than the obvious one.

'Maybe Rourke just changed his mind——'

'No way,' Gene laughed. 'Never in a million years. There are some women who just turn you off, Clare, and your mother did that to Rourke.'

'But he's going to direct her next film!'

'When he will be firmly in charge. Your mother knows that very well. But Rourke is *the* director of the moment, so your mother will behave herself.'

'I see.' But she didn't see at all, couldn't understand any of this. Had her mother lied to her? Why not, it sounded as if lying to achieve her objective was the least she would do.

'There's something else I think you should know about Rourke,' Gene said slowly.

'Yes?' her voice was sharp.

'His—lack of interest in women has caused a lot of speculation the last few years, so much so that there've even been rumours that women no longer interest him—if you know what I mean.'

Delicate colour flooded her cheeks. 'No one could seriously believe *that* about Rourke?' she gasped.

'Not really,' Gene laughed. 'I mean, I know it isn't true——'

'You mean he hasn't made a pass at you,' she taunted.

'No, I didn't mean that,' he sighed. 'But Rourke's complete turnaround came as something of a shock after—well, after——'

'After having a different woman in his bed almost every night,' Clare finished derisively.

'Don't be bitchy, Clare,' he chided softly. 'And he wasn't that bad.'

'Rumour has it——'

'Rumour has a lot of things, and most of them untrue. Now, I'm going back to the dance, maybe I can impress Little Miss Sex-bomb with the fact that my father owns a studio. Maybe she'll even invite me back to her room,' Gene added eagerly.

'I wouldn't be at all surprised,' Clare said bitterly.

'And you should talk to Rourke the first chance you get,' he told her seriously.

A shutter came down over her features. 'Rourke doesn't think we have anything left to say to each other.'

'And you know that isn't true. At least give him the chance you didn't give him five years ago, to explain himself.'

Her mouth twisted. 'I doubt Rourke has ever thought he had to explain himself to anyone—least of all me.'

Gene bent and kissed her briefly on the lips. 'I'd hate
you to lose your chance of happiness because of pride.'

She bit her lip. 'What do you think I should do?'

'You really want to know?'

'Yes,' she said huskily.

'Okay,' he nodded. 'Then I think you should go back
and claim your man.'

'Like a bounty hunter?' she taunted to hide her ner-
vousness. Go back there and face Rourke, ask to speak
to him? Could she do it? Could what Gene had told her
really make that much difference? Rourke hadn't exactly
been encouraging the morning after they made love. But
what if she had misjudged that too?

'Like a bounty hunter,' Gene agreed. 'Are you
prepared to do that?'

'I—I don't know.'

'God, what does it take, Clare?' He was angry now.
'A sworn declaration from Rourke that nothing
happened between him and your mother?'

'No, of course not——'

'Then for God's sake do something about this mess!'

She straightened her shoulders, coming to a decision.
'I'll talk to him. Things can't be any worse between us
than they are now.'

'Good girl!' Gene took her by the arm, going back in
the direction of the music. 'And don't worry about
Belinda, I'll take care of her.'

Belinda was the last person she was worried about!
Rourke just might not want to talk to her! 'I'm sure
that will be a hardship,' she vaguely teased Gene.

'Oh yes,' he grinned, going straight towards the other
couple as they still danced together. 'Can I cut in?' he
repeated Rourke's comment of minutes earlier.

'Sure,' Rourke drawled. 'I——' He had turned and
seen Clare, and his face stiffened. 'If you'll excuse me!'
He turned and walked away.

'Go to it, Clare!' Gene whispered in her ear.

Her movements were jerky, and she didn't seem to be

making any progress on Rourke as he strode away. She
finally had to call out to him, seeing him stiffen as he
heard her.

He turned slowly, his eyes narrowed. 'Yes?'

His tone wasn't forthcoming, and she licked her lips
nervously. 'I—I wanted to talk to you.'

'Yes?' His tone was even chillier.

It wasn't pride that was holding her back, it was fear,
fear of having Rourke reject her for a second time.
'Rourke—Rourke——'

'For God's sake spit it out, Clare,' he said impatiently.
'I need to get a drink.'

'Could we talk—somewhere more private?' She pulled
a face at the sound of the music.

He seemed to hesitate. 'I guess so,' he finally nodded.
'Your boy-friend seems to be disappearing with Belinda.'

Clare turned just in time for Gene to wink at her as
he and Belinda disappeared into the darkness. 'Do you
mind?' she asked Rourke breathlessly.

'Do you?'

'Not in the least,' she answered truthfully.

Rourke's eyes narrowed. 'You don't?'

'No,' she shook her head, feeling as if they were the
only two people in the world. 'You misunderstood what
you saw earlier, Gene was merely showering and changing. We hadn't been to bed together.'

There was an air of tension about him now. 'No?'

'No. Rourke, could we please talk? Please!'

His breathing was ragged. 'I never could resist you
when you said please.'

'You did once,' she remembered with pain.

'Because I could see you with Pryce!' His expression
was savage.

'Harvey's gone, Rourke,' she told him.

'Gone?' he echoed sharply. 'But he'll be back?'

'No. He—he got married this afternoon.'

'Married? What the hell——! The two of you got
married this afternoon?'

Was it her imagination or had he gone grey under his tan? 'I said Harvey got married, Rourke,' she said gently, hope starting to lighten her heart. 'Harvey married someone else.'

He grasped her arm. 'You're right, we need to talk. Shall we go back to our room?'

'Our' room! God, that sounded so intimate—and so right. 'Yes,' she agreed without hesitation.

For once they entered through Rourke's suite. 'Sit down,' he invited gruffly. 'Now tell me about Pryce,' he instructed abruptly.

'He—he married Shara Morgan earlier today. They're in Las Vegas.'

'Shara Morgan?' Rourke frowned. 'Where the hell does she come into all this?'

Clare explained about Harvey's past relationship with the other woman. 'They just realised they still loved each other,' she shrugged.

'I see,' he said slowly. 'Thanks for telling me. I'll try to make allowances for your unhappiness——'

'Oh, but I'm not unhappy,' she interrupted firmly.

His eyes narrowed. 'You aren't?'

'No,' she shook her head. 'I wasn't going to marry him anyway.'

'You weren't?'

He wasn't really helping her very much, but then why should he, he had no idea what she was trying to lead up to. She licked her lips nervously, stopping the movement as she realised he was watching her. 'Rourke, five years ago I—I was in love with you——'

'Yes.'

Her eyes widened. 'You knew?'

'Of course I knew,' he snapped. 'You weren't the type of girl to go to bed with a man you didn't love—not then, anyway,' he added bitterly.

'Not now, either,' she told him softly.

He put up a hand to his temple, as if it ached, a look

of strain about his eyes and mouth. 'What does all this have to do with the fact that your fiancé married someone else?'

'Nothing.'

'Nothing . . .? Then what the hell——'

'But it has everything to do with the fact that I also *left* Los Angeles five years ago because I loved you.'

His mouth twisted. 'Now that isn't true. You left because you couldn't stand the sight of me. And I can't blame you.'

'Where on earth did you get that idea?' she frowned. 'Of course that wasn't the reason I left.'

'You couldn't stand for me to touch you,' he rasped bleakly.

'I—But—I—Are you saying *I* was the exception?'

'The one who didn't purr?' he derided. 'You know damn well you didn't—you cried.'

'Cried? But——'

'It's no good, Clare,' he turned to look out of the porthole. 'You cried, and I knew I couldn't give you physical pleasure. The first time—God, the first time I was completely out of control, unable to stop even though I knew I was hurting you. The second time—the second time——'

'You said you didn't remember the second time,' she said softly.

He didn't turn; his back was rigid. 'I tried not to, but I never could forget it. I let you down——'

'No——'

'Yes,' he sighed wearily.

'You didn't let *me* down, *I* disappointed you,' she frowned.

'Like hell you did!' Rourke turned now, his eyes glittering with emotion. 'You never ever disappointed me. I loved every minute I spent with you. I loved your fresh approach to life, your spontaneity, the way you never tried to pretend. You were you, Clare Anderson, the girl I laughed with, played with,' he paused, hesitating.

'Cried with,' he added so softly she could hardly hear him.

She blinked dazedly, sure she must have misheard. 'What did you say?'

'I'm sure you heard me,' he said bitterly.

'I—I think I did,' she nodded, frowning. 'Did you say *cried* with?'

'Yes,' he snapped harshly. 'I hurt the girl I loved, of course I cried.'

Clare gulped. 'The girl you loved . . .?'

His eyes flashed deeply blue. 'Yes, God damn you! I hurt you, I let you down. The one woman I wanted above all others I couldn't even give physical pleasure to.'

Clare shook her head. 'That isn't true!'

'Of course it is. You even told your mother how I disgusted you. She passed your message on word for word, Clare, and I bled with each one of them,' he revealed in a pained voice.

Her mother! Oh God, her mother! 'Rourke,' she chewed on her bottom lip, 'five years ago——'

'Could we forget the past?' he rasped. 'What good does it do to talk about it? It's over, finished.'

He looked so bleak, so utterly defeated, that she knew she had to go to him. She moved as if in a daze, her arms going about his waist, her head resting on his chest. Rourke didn't move, standing rigid and unyielding. Finally she looked up at him, touching his cheek with loving tenderness.

His jaw tightened even more. 'What are you trying to do to me?' he muttered.

'I'm trying, not very successfully I'll admit, to tell you I love you, that I've always loved you.'

Rourke's breath caught in his throat at the steady, trusting way she gazed up at him. 'I don't understand——'

'Do you love me?'

'Clare——'

'Do you?'

'God, yes!' he groaned, his arms at last coming up about her waist, drawing her closer. 'I always have. For five years I've been haunted by you. You've been like a fever in my blood, a golden fever,' he touched her hair wonderingly. 'Everything about you glittering and pure. And you ruined me for other women.'

'And Gene thought you had suddenly decided you preferred men,' she teased, a warm glow spreading through her body at the wonderful things Rourke was telling her, at his possessive hold on her.

'He thought *what*?' Rourke exploded.

'Don't worry,' she chuckled. 'I soon told him he was mistaken.'

'I should damn well hope so,' he scowled. 'I was in love with you, I didn't want anyone else,' he revealed candidly. 'And it was five years of torture.'

'Oh, Rourke,' she shivered. 'What did she do to us?' she groaned.

'She?'

'My mother,' she said huskily.

'Your mother?' He stiffened, holding her away from him. 'Are you telling me she lied to me, that I've suffered the tortures of hell for nothing?'

'Yes.'

He seemed to shake with rage, and then he frowned. 'But you did cry, and you did leave . . .'

'I cried because I was so overwhelmed by what had happened between us. I—It was beautiful, everything I'd ever imagined, and I just reacted by crying. I couldn't help myself. As to why I left . . .' she paused.

Rourke's fingers tightened on her arms. 'Your mother did something else, didn't she? Tell me, Clare,' he ordered.

She licked her lips. 'After you left the beach-house to go to work I just wanted to die. I felt—I felt used.'

'No!'

'But I did,' she shuddered. 'You left so abruptly,

almost as if you couldn't bear to be near me. I went
home. I was numb, and when Gene asked me out I
went, to show you you didn't matter to me either.'

'I didn't go to work that day, Clare,' he interrupted
quietly. 'I went to the house in Bel Air. And I got
stoned—out of my mind. When I telephoned your home
your mother said you were out, with Gene. I must have
called half a dozen times throughout the evening. I
finally came to the conclusion that your mother was
lying to me, so I went over there. I had some crazy idea
of finding you if I had to pull the place apart,' he said
ruefully. 'I got as far as the bedrooms before I passed
out on the floor.'

'My mother's bedroom,' she put in huskily.

'Was it? I don't know. I don't remember a thing after
I passed out.'

'You were put in the bed,' she told him jerkily.

'Oh, I know that. Charles told me——'

'Charles?' she echoed sharply.

'Mm. Apparently he was the one who put me there.'

'In my mother's bed,' Clare said again, more
pointedly this time.

'So you said,' Rourke nodded. 'But—My God!' he
seemed to pale. 'She didn't let you think—She couldn't
have——'

'She did,' she said dully.

'She told you—You thought—That's why you went
to England?' he gasped.

'Yes,' she choked.

His expression was fierce. 'She must be sick——'

Clare shook her head. 'She wanted you. Even I might
go to those lengths to get you.'

'Do you want me?' he asked huskily.

'Oh yes!' she answered without reserve.

'Enough to marry me?'

'More than enough.' Her eyes glowed.

'Sweetheart . . .!' he groaned, his mouth claiming hers
in a kiss of infinite sweetness.

Clare kissed him back with all of the love inside her, pouting her disappointment when he put her away from him.

'Not until we're married,' he teased, the lines of strain leaving his eyes and mouth.

She snuggled into his body. 'Then perhaps we'd better follow Harvey's example and go to Las Vegas.'

'No.' Rourke shook his head firmly.

'No?' she pulled a face.

'I want us to be married here, by the Captain.'

'He can still do that?' Her eyes lit up with excitement.

'Mm,' Rourke nodded, love shining in his eyes. 'They often have weddings on board, in the chapel.'

'I've seen it, it's beautiful.'

'Yes,' he touched her face with tenderness. 'Like you. And I want you to have the perfect wedding.'

And they did. The whole film crew was there, Gene accompanying Belinda, the two of them obviously very friendly. Harvey and the lovely Shara were present too, looking ecstatically happy together.

The chapel looked beautiful, full of white flowers and flowing white ribbons, the small chapel giving the wedding an intimate atmosphere.

'I'm not sure the colour was appropriate,' Clare said ruefully later that evening once they had retired to their suite for the night, only one of the bedrooms being used tonight. Rourke had kept to his decision that they wouldn't make love until they were married, and so the anticipation of their night ahead together was two-fold.

'Of course it was,' he nuzzled into her throat. 'My only regret is that I can't see your mother's face when she finds out we've got married despite all her machinations.'

Her mother hadn't even been invited to the wedding, in fact it hadn't even been mentioned that they should invite her. Clare frowned. 'I'm not looking forward to you working with her,' she said worriedly.

His eyes darkened several shades deeper. 'Believe me, Clare, by that time you'll be so sure of your own power over me that you won't feel a qualm. Your mother means nothing to me, she never has.'

She could feel the arousal of his body for her and knew it was the truth. Rourke was hers as surely as she was his. 'Did you really cancel *Gun Serenade* so that you could work with me?' She traced the outline of his lips with her fingertips.

'I really did,' he admitted ruefully. 'I wanted to see you again badly, but I couldn't just appear, I had to have a valid reason for being where you were. I jumped at the chance of working with you. Although it turned out to be agony. You belonged to Pryce, or so I thought, and all I could do was hurt you with my insulting comments. To my shame I was even brutal about making love to you before, just to save my own pride. After just two days I was wishing I'd never come here.'

'And now?'

'Now I'm going to take you to bed,' he swung her up into his arms, 'and I doubt either of us will sleep until morning.'

'Mm, sounds wonderful!' Clare leant her head on his shoulder. 'What are you smiling at?' she asked suspiciously at the twinkling mischief in his eyes.

'I wonder if any other man has had to do nude scenes for a movie, with his wife, while still on his honeymoon?' He laughed at her fiery blushes. 'It could be pornographic!'

She put her arms up about his neck, kissing his throat, biting his earlobe, the nude scenes they were to do together no longer bothering her. 'I'll just have to make sure you're too exhausted tomorrow to do anything but act.'

His mouth quirked. 'I have a five-year thirst to satisfy, it would take more than one night with you to do that. I'm hoping it will take a lifetime.'

'I'll see that it does,' she murmured throatily,

momentarily touching the gold medallion Rourke had given her from around his own neck in lieu of an engagement ring. The medallion meant more to her than any ring could ever do, signifying that Rourke no longer needed his independence, that he had given his life and happiness into her keeping as surely as she had given him hers. 'I love you, Mr Somerville,' she told him with a catch in her throat.

'I love you too, Mrs Somerville. Now would you mind if I made love to my wife?'

'I'd love it!' Clare gave him a glowing smile.

'And this time, this time,' he said seriously. 'Make no mistake about how much I enjoy it, how much I love you. I could never stand to lose you again,' his arms tightened about her.

'You're never going to,' she promised as she arched her body into his, her lips parting for his kiss.

Harlequin Plus

A SCANDALOUS ROMANCE

History has many famous romantic twosomes, whose stories have become almost legends, touching the hearts of all who hear them. One such is the tragic love story of Lord Nelson and Lady Hamilton.

Born the son of a country parson, Horatio Nelson went to sea in 1770, when he was twelve. A born leader, he became a national hero in Britain after winning the Battle of the Nile against Napoleon's navy. Admiral Nelson was said to have aroused the affection of all who met him—from common sailor to king.

Similarly, Emma Hamilton was known for her grace and charm—and also as one of the great beauties of her time. She was born in 1761, the daughter of a blacksmith, and from these humble origins rose to become an actress, singer, an inspiration to painters and the confidante of aristocrats and politicians.

Lord Nelson met Lady Hamilton in Italy in 1793, and although they were both already married, they fell deeply in love. It was not an age that looked kindly on such liaisons, yet despite accusations of scandal, both stood loyal to each other—and proud of their love. She bore his child in secrecy while he was away at sea, and when scandalmongers tried to intercept their letters, the pair continued to write under assumed names.

Nelson called Emma, "all that I hold dear in this world." Yet when duty called, he returned to sea in 1805 to fight Napoleon's navy at Trafalgar. Nelson won the battle but lost his life.

The distraught Lady Hamilton continued to endure with great courage and dignity the many people who scorned her. She died, ten years later, poor and in exile in France. But her love for Nelson never wavered and remains an example of the devotion that only the strongest and deepest of loves can engender.

Introducing...

Harlequin American Romance

An exciting new series of sensuous and emotional love stories—contemporary, engrossing and uniquely American. Long, satisfying novels of conflict and challenge, stories of modern men and women dealing with life and love in today's changing world.

Get to know
Harlequin Reader Service

**Complete and mail
this coupon for
your FREE
catalog today!**

Take these 4 best-selling novels FREE

ANNE MATHER
born out of love

VIOLET WINSPEAR
time of the temptress

CHARLOTTE LAMB
man's world

SALLY WENTWORTH
say hello to yesterday

Take these 4 best-selling novels FREE

as advertised on TV

Yes! Four sophisticated, contemporary love stories by four world-famous authors of romance FREE, as your introduction to the Harlequin Presents subscription plan. Thrill to **Anne Mather**'s passionate story BORN OUT OF LOVE, set in the Caribbean…. Travel to darkest Africa in **Violet Winspear**'s TIME OF THE TEMPTRESS…. Let **Charlotte Lamb** take you to the fascinating world of London's Fleet Street in MAN'S WORLD…. Discover beautiful Greece in **Sally Wentworth**'s moving romance SAY HELLO TO YESTERDAY.

Harlequin Presents…

The very finest in romance fiction

Join the millions of avid Harlequin readers all over the world who delight in the magic of a really exciting novel. EIGHT great NEW titles published EACH MONTH! Each month you will get to know exciting, interesting, true-to-life people …. You'll be swept to distant lands you've dreamed of visiting …. Intrigue, adventure, romance, and the destiny of many lives will thrill you through each Harlequin Presents novel.

Get all the latest books before they're sold out!
As a Harlequin subscriber you actually receive your personal copies of the latest Presents novels immediately after they come off the press, so you're sure of getting all 8 each month.

Cancel your subscription whenever you wish!
You don't have to buy any minimum number of books. Whenever you decide to stop your subscription just let us know and we'll cancel all further shipments.